Michael Moorcock is astonishing. His enormous output includes around sixty novels, innumerable short stories and a rock album. Born in London in 1939, he became editor of *Tarzan Adventures* at sixteen, moving on later to edit the *Sexton Blake Library*. He has earned his living as a writer/editor ever since, and is without doubt one of Britain's most popular and most prolific authors. He has been compared with Tennyson, Tolkien, Raymond Chandler, Wyndham Lewis, Ronald Firbank, Mervyn Peake, Edgar Allan Poe, Colin Wilson, Anatole France, William Burroughs, Edgar Rice Burroughs, Charles Dickens, James Joyce, Vladimir Nabokov, Jorge Luis Borges, Joyce Cary, Ray Bradbury, H. G. Wells, George Bernard Shaw and Hieronymus Bosch, among others.

'No one at the moment in England is doing more to break down the artificial divisions that have grown up in novel writing – realism, surrealism, science fiction, historical fiction, social satire, the poetic novel – than Michael Moorcock'
Angus Wilson

'He is an ingenious and energetic experimenter, restlessly original, brimming over with clever ideas'
Robert Nye, *The Guardian*

For further information about the works of Michael Moorcock, write to:–

> The Nomads of the Time Streams
> (The Michael Moorcock Appreciation Society)
> PO Box 451048
> Atlanta
> Georgia 30345–1048
> USA

By the same author

The Cornelius Chronicles
The Final Programme
A Cure for Cancer
The English Assassin
The Condition of Muzak
The Lives and Times of Jerry Cornelius
The Adventures of Una Persson and Catherine Cornelius in the Twentieth Century

The Dancers at the End of Time
An Alien Heat
The Hollow Lands
The End of All Songs
Legends from the End of Time
The Transformation of Miss Mavis Ming (Return of the Fireclown)

Hawkmoon: The History of the Runestaff
The Jewel in the Skull
The Mad God's Amulet
The Sword of the Dawn
The Runestaff

Hawkmoon: The Chronicles of Castle Brass
Count Brass
The Champion of Garathorm
The Quest for Tanelorn

Erekosë
The Eternal Champion
Phoenix in Obsidian
The Dragon in the Sword

Elric
Elric of Melniboné
The Sailor on the Seas of Fate
The Weird of the White Wolf
The Vanishing Tower
Stormbringer
Elric at the End of Time
The Fortress of the Pearl

The Books of Corum
The Knight of the Swords
The Queen of the Swords
The King of the Swords
The Bull and the Spear
The Oak and the Ram
The Sword and the Stallion

Michael Kane
The City of the Beast
The Lord of the Spiders
The Masters of the Pit

The Nomad of Time
The War Lord of the Air
The Land Leviathan
The Steel Tsar

Other Titles
The Winds of Limbo
The Ice Schooner
Behold the Man
Breakfast in the Ruins
The Blood-Red Game
The Black Corridor
The Chinese Agent
The Russian Intelligence
The Distant Suns
The Rituals of Infinity
The Shores of Death
Sojan the Swordsman (juvenile)
The Golden Barge
Gloriana (or, The Unfulfill'd Queene, a Romance)
The Time Dweller (short stories)
Moorcock's Book of Martyrs (short stories)
The Entropy Tango
Wizardry and Wild Romance (non-fiction)
Byzantium Endures
The Laughter of Carthage
The Brothel in Rosenstrasse
The War Hound and the World's Pain
The City in the Autumn Stars
Letters from Hollywood (non-fiction)
The Opium General (short stories)
Mother London

MICHAEL MOORCOCK

The Bane of the Black Sword

GRAFTON BOOKS
A Division of the Collins Publishing Group

LONDON GLASGOW
TORONTO SYDNEY AUCKLAND

Grafton Books
A Division of the Collins Publishing Group
8 Grafton Street, London W1X 3LA

Published by Panther Books 1984
Reprinted 1984 (twice), 1989, 1990 (twice)

ISBN 0-586-06230-0

Part of this book originally appeared in a volume
entitled *The Stealer of Souls*. This revised version
contains a section never previously published in
chronological sequence but which appeared out of
context in a collection entitled *The Singing Citadel*.
This is the first time this revised edition has been
published in the British Commonwealth.

Printed and bound in Great Britain by
Collins, Glasgow

Set in Times

To the memory of Hans Stefan Santesson, an editor of great patience and kindness who, with L. Sprague de Camp, encouraged me in the late 1950s to write heroic fantasy. His magazine, *Fantastic Universe*, ceased publication before I could contribute, much to my regret, for it was, in my opinion, one of the best fantasy magazines ever produced.

BOOK ONE

The Stealer of Souls

In which Elric once again makes the acquaintance of Queen Yishana of Jharkor and Theleb K'aarna of Pan Tang and receives satisfaction at last.

1

In a city called Bakshaan, which was rich enough to make all other cities of the North East seem poor, in a tall-towered tavern one night, Elric, Lord of the smoking ruins of Melniboné, smiled like a shark and dryly jested with four powerful merchant princes whom, in a day or so, he intended to pauperize.

Moonglum the Outlander, Elric's companion, viewed the tall albino with admiration and concern. For Elric to laugh and joke was rare but that he should share his good humour with men of the merchant stamp, that was unprecedented. Moonglum congratulated himself that he was Elric's friend and wondered upon the outcome of the meeting. Elric had, as usual, elaborated little of his plan to Moonglum.

'We need your particular qualities as swordsman and sorcerer, Lord Elric, and will, of course, pay well for them.' Pilarmo, overdressed, intense and scrawny, was main spokesman for the four.

'And how shall you pay, gentlemen?' inquired Elric politely, still smiling.

Pilarmo's colleagues raised their eyebrows and even their spokesman was slightly taken aback. He waved his hand through the smoky air of the tavern-room which was occupied only by the six men.

'In gold – in gems,' answered Pilarmo.

'In chains,' said Elric. 'We free travellers need no chains of that sort.'

Moonglum bent forward out of the shadows where he sat, his expression showing that he strongly disapproved of Elric's statement.

Pilarmo and the other merchants were plainly astonished, too. 'Then how shall we pay you?'

'I will decide that later,' Elric smiled. 'But why talk of such things until the time – what do you wish me to do?'

Pilarmo coughed and exchanged glances with his peers. They nodded. Pilarmo dropped his tone and spoke slowly:

'You are aware that trade is highly competitive in this city, Lord Elric. Many merchants vie with one another to secure the custom of the people. Bakshaan is a rich city and its populace is comfortably off, in the main.'

'This is well known,' Elric agreed; he was privately likening the well-to-do citizens of Bakshaan to sheep and himself to the wolf who would rob the fold. Because of these thoughts, his scarlet eyes were full of a humour which Moonglum knew to be malevolent and ironic.

'There is one merchant in this city who controls more warehouses and shops than any other,' Pilarmo continued. 'Because of the size and strength of his caravans, he can afford to import greater quantities of goods into Bakshaan and thus sell them for lower prices. He is virtually a thief – he will ruin us with his unfair methods.' Pilarmo was genuinely hurt and aggrieved.

'You refer to Nikorn of Ilmar?' Moonglum spoke from behind Elric.

Pilarmo nodded mutely.

Elric frowned. 'This man heads his own caravans – braves the dangers of the desert, forest and mountain. He has earned his position.'

'That is hardly the point,' snapped fat Tormiel, beringed and powdered, his flesh a-quiver.

'No, of course not.' Smooth-tongued Kelos patted his colleague's arm consolingly. 'But we all admire bravery, I hope.' His friends nodded. Silent Deinstaf, the last of the four, also coughed and wagged his hairy head. He put his unhealthy fingers on the jewelled hilt of an ornate but virtually useless poignard and squared his shoulders. 'But,' Kelos went on, glancing at Deinstaf with approval, 'Nikorn takes no risks selling his goods cheaply – he's killing us with

10

his low prices.'

'Nikorn is a thorn in our flesh,' Pilarmo elaborated unnecessarily.

'And you gentlemen require myself and my companion to remove this thorn,' Elric stated.

'In a nutshell, yes.' Pilarmo was sweating. He seemed more than a trifle wary of the smiling albino. Legends referring to Elric and his dreadful, doom-filled exploits were many and elaborately detailed. It was only because of their desperation that they had sought his help in this matter. They needed one who could deal in the nigromantic arts as well as wield a useful blade. Elric's arrival in Bakshaan was potential salvation for them.

'We wish to destroy Nikorn's power,' Pilarmo continued. 'And if this means destroying Nikorn, then –' He shrugged and half-smiled, watching Elric's face.

'Common assassins are easily employed, particularly in Bakshaan,' Elric pointed out softly.

'Uh – true,' Pilarmo agreed. 'But Nikorn employs a sorcerer – and a private army. The sorcerer protects him and his palace by means of magic. And a guard of desertmen serve to ensure that if magic fails, then natural methods can be used for the purpose. Assassins have attempted to eliminate the trader, but unfortunately, they were not lucky.'

Elric laughed. 'How disappointing, my friends. Still, assassins are the most dispensable members of the community – are they not? And their souls probably went to placate some demon who would otherwise have plagued more honest folk.'

The merchants laughed half-heartedly and, at this, Moonglum grinned, enjoying himself from his seat in the shadows.

Elric poured wine for the other five. It was of a vintage which the law in Bakshaan forbade the populace from drinking. Too much drove the imbiber mad, yet Elric had already quaffed great quantities and showed no ill effects. He raised a cup of the yellow wine to his lips and drained it, breathing deeply and with satisfaction as the stuff entered his system. The others sipped theirs cautiously. The merchants were already regretting their haste in contacting the albino. They had a feeling that not only were the legends true – but they did not do justice to the strange-eyed man they wished to employ.

Elric poured more yellow wine into his goblet and his hand trembled slightly and his dry tongue moved over his lips quickly. His breathing increased as he allowed the beverage to trickle down his throat. He had taken more than enough to make other men into mewling idiots, but those few signs were the only indication that the wine had any effect upon him at all.

This was a wine for those who wished to dream of different and less tangible worlds. Elric drank it in the hope that he would, for a night or so, cease to dream.

Now he asked: 'And who is this mighty sorcerer, Master Pilarmo?'

'His name is Theleb K'aarna,' Pilarmo answered nervously.

Elric's scarlet eyes narrowed. 'The sorcerer of Pan Tang?'

'Aye – he comes from that island.'

Elric put his cup down upon the table and rose, fingering his blade of black iron, the runesword Stormbringer.

He said with conviction: 'I will help you, gentlemen.' He had made up his mind not to rob them, after all. A new and more important plan was forming in his brain.

'Theleb K'aarna,' he thought. *'So you have made Bakshaan your bolt-hole, eh?'*

Theleb K'aarna tittered. It was an obscene sound, coming as it did from the throat of a sorcerer of no mean skill. It did not fit with his sombre, black-bearded countenance, his tall, scarlet-robed frame. It was not a sound suited to one of his extreme wisdom.

Theleb K'aarna tittered and stared with dreamy eyes at the woman who lolled on the couch beside him. He whispered clumsy words of endearment into her ear and she smiled indulgently, stroking his long, black hair as she would stroke the coat of a dog.

'You're a fool, for all your learning, Theleb K'aarna,' she murmured, her hooded eyes staring beyond him at the bright green and orange tapestries which decorated the stone walls of her bed-chamber. She reflected lazily that a woman could not but help take advantage of any man who put himself so into her power.

'Yishana, you are a bitch,' Theleb K'aarna breathed foolishly, 'and all the learning in the world cannot combat love. I love you.' He spoke simply, directly, not understanding the woman who lay beside him. He had seen into the black bowels of hell and had returned sane, he knew secrets which would turn any ordinary man's mind into quivering, jumbled jelly. But in certain arts he was as unversed as his youngest acolyte. The art of love was one of those. 'I love you,' he repeated, and wondered why she ignored him.

Yishana, Queen of Jharkor, pushed the sorcerer away from her and rose abruptly, swinging bare, well-formed legs off the divan. She was a handsome woman, with hair as black as her soul; though her youth was fading, she had a strange quality about her which both repelled and attracted men. She wore her multi-coloured silks well and they swirled about her as, with light grace, she strode to the barred window of the chamber and stared out into the dark and turbulent night. The sorcerer watched her through narrow, puzzled eyes, disappointed at this halt to their lovemaking.

'What's wrong?'

The Queen continued to stare out at the night. Great banks of black cloud moved like predatory monsters, swiftly across the wind-torn sky. The night was raucous and

13

angry about Bakshaan; full of ominous portent.

Theleb K'aarna repeated his question and again received no answer. He stood up angrily, then, and joined her at the window.

'Let us leave now, Yishana, before it is too late. If Elric learns of our presence in Bakshaan, we shall both suffer.' She did not reply, but her breasts heaved beneath the flimsy fabric and her mouth tightened.

The sorcerer growled, gripping her arm. 'Forget your renegade freebooter, Elric – you have me now, and I can do much more for you than any sword-swinging medicine-man from a broken and senile empire!'

Yishana laughed unpleasantly and turned on her lover. 'You are a fool, Theleb K'aarna, and you're much less of a man than Elric. Three aching years have passed since he deserted me, skulking off into the night on your trail and leaving me to pine for him! But I still remember his savage kisses and his wild love-making. Gods! I wish he had an equal. Since he left, I've never found one to match him – though many have tried and proved better than you – until you came skulking back and your spells drove them off or destroyed them.' She sneered, mocking and taunting him. 'You've been too long among your parchments to be much good to me!'

The sorcerer's face muscles tautened beneath his tanned skin and he scowled. 'Then why do you let me remain? I could make you my slave with a potion – you know that!'

'But you wouldn't – and are thus *my* slave, mighty wizard. When Elric threatened to displace you in my affections, you conjured that demon and Elric was forced to fight it. He won you'll remember – but in his pride refused to compromise. You fled into hiding and he went in search of you – leaving me! That is what you did. You're in *love*, Theleb K'aarna . . .' she laughed in his face. 'And your love won't let you use your arts against me – only my other lovers. I put up with you because you are often useful, but if Elric were to return . . .'

Theleb K'aarna turned away, pettishly picking at his long black beard. Yishana said: 'I half hate Elric, aye! But that is better than half loving you!'

The sorcerer snarled: 'Then why did you join me in Bakshaan? Why did you leave your brother's son upon your throne as regent and come here? I sent word and you came – you must have some affection for me to do that!'

Yishana laughed again. 'I heard that a pale-faced sorcerer with crimson eyes and a howling runesword was travelling in the North East. That is why I came, Theleb K'aarna.'

Theleb K'aarna's face twisted with anger as he bent forward and gripped the woman's shoulder in his taloned hand.

'You'll remember that this same pale-faced sorcerer was responsible for your own brother's death,' he spat. 'You lay with a man who was a slayer of his kin and yours. He deserted the fleet, which he had led to pillage his own land, when the Dragon Masters retaliated. Dharmit, your brother, was aboard one of those ships and he now lies scorched and rotting on the ocean bed.'

Yishana shook her head wearily. 'You always mention this and hope to shame me. Yes, I entertained one who was virtually my brother's murderer – but Elric had ghastlier crimes on his conscience and I still loved him, in spite or because of them. Your words do not have the effect you require, Theleb K'aarna. Now leave me, I wish to sleep alone.'

The sorcerer's nails were still biting into Yishana's cool flesh. He relaxed his grip. 'I am sorry,' he said, his voice breaking. 'Let me stay.'

'Go,' she said softly. And, tortured by his own weakness, Theleb K'aarna, sorcerer of Pan Tang, left. Elric of Melniboné was in Bakshaan – and Elric had sworn several oaths of vengeance upon Theleb K'aarna on several separate occasions – in Lormyr, Nadsokor and Taueloru, as well as in Jharkor. In his heart, the black-bearded sorcerer knew who would win any duel which might take place.

2

The four merchants had left swathed in dark cloaks. They had not deemed it wise for anyone to be aware of their association with Elric. Now, Elric brooded over a fresh cup of yellow wine. He knew that he would need help of a particular and powerful kind, if he were going to capture Nikorn's castle. It was virtually unstormable and, with Theleb K'aarna's nigromantic protection, a particularly potent sorcery would have to be used. He knew that he was Theleb K'aarna's match and more when it came to wizardry, but if all his energy were expended on fighting the other magician, he would have none left to effect an entry past the crack guard of desert warriors employed by the merchant prince.

He needed help. In the forests which lay to the south of Bakshaan, he knew he would find men whose aid would be useful. But would they help him? He discussed the problem with Moonglum.

'I have heard that a band of my countrymen have recently come north from Vilmir where they have pillaged several large towns,' he informed the Eastlander. 'Since the great battle of Imrryr four years ago, the men of Melniboné have spread outwards from the Dragon Isle, becoming mercenaries and freebooters. It was because of me that Imrryr fell – and this they know, but if I offer them rich loot, they might aid me.'

Moonglum smiled wryly. 'I would not count on it, Elric,' he said. 'Such an act as yours can hardly be forgotten, if you'll forgive my frankness. Your countrymen are now unwilling wanderers, citizens of a razed city – the oldest and greatest the world has known. When Imrryr the Beautiful fell, there must have been many who wished great suffering

17

upon you.'

Elric emitted a short laugh. 'Possibly,' he agreed, 'but these *are* my people and I know them. We Melnibonéans are an old and sophisticated race – we rarely allow emotions to interfere with our general well-being.'

Moonglum raised his eyebrows in an ironic grimace and Elric interpreted the expression rightly. 'I was an exception for a short while,' he said. 'But now Cymoril and my cousin lie in the ruins of Imrryr and my own torment will avenge any ill I have done. I think my countrymen will realize this.'

Moonglum sighed. 'I hope you are right, Elric. Who leads this band?'

'An old friend,' Elric answered. 'He was Dragon Master and led the attack upon the reaver ships after they had looted Imrryr. His name is Dyvim Tvar, once Lord of the Dragon Caves.'

'And what of his beasts, where are they?'

'Asleep in the caves again. They can be roused only rarely – they need years to recuperate while their venom is re-distilled and their energy revitalized. If it were not for this, the Dragon Masters would rule the world.'

'Lucky for you that they don't,' Moonglum commented.

Elric said slowly: 'Who knows? With me to lead them, they might yet. At least, we could carve a new empire from this world, just as our forefathers did.'

Moonglum said nothing. He thought, privately, that the Young Kingdoms would not be so easily vanquished. Melniboné and her people were ancient, cruel and wise – but even their cruelty was tempered with the soft disease which comes with age. They lacked the vitality of the barbarian race who had been the ancestors of the builders of Imrryr and her long-forgotten sister cities. Vitality was often replaced by tolerance – the tolerance of the aged, the ones who have known past glory but whose day is done.

'In the morning,' said Elric, 'we will make contact with Dyvim Tvar and hope that what he did to the reaver fleet, coupled with the conscience-pangs which I have personally suffered, will serve to give him a properly objective attitude to my scheme.'

'And now, sleep, I think,' Moonglum said. 'I need it, anyway – and the wench who awaits me might be growing impatient.'

Elric shrugged. 'As you will. I'll drink a little more wine and seek my bed later.'

The black clouds which had huddled over Bakshaan on the previous night, were still there in the morning. The sun rose behind them, but the inhabitants were unaware of it. It rose unheralded, but in the fresh, rain-splashed dawn, Elric and Moonglum rode the narrow streets of the city, heading for the south gate and the forests beyond.

Elric had discarded his usual garb for a simple jerkin of green-dyed leather which bore the insignia of the royal line of Melniboné: a scarlet dragon, rampant on a gold field. On his finger was the Ring of Kings, the single rare Actorious stone set in a ring of rune-carved silver. This was the ring that Elric's mighty forefathers had worn; it was many centuries old. A short cloak hung from his shoulders and his hose was also blue, tucked into high black riding boots. At his side hung Stormbringer.

A symbiosis existed between man and sword. The man without the sword could become a cripple, lacking sight and energy – the sword without the man could not drink the blood and the souls it needed for its existence. They rode together, sword and man, and none could tell which was master.

Moonglum, more conscious of the inclement weather than his friend, hugged a high-collared cloak around him and cursed the elements occasionally.

It took them an hour's hard riding to reach the outskirts of the forest. As yet, in Bakshaan, there were only rumours of the Imrryrian freebooters' coming. Once or twice, a tall stranger had been seen in obscure taverns near the southern wall, and this had been remarked upon but the citizens of Bakshaan felt secure in their wealth and power and had reasoned, with a certain truth in their conviction, that Bakshaan could withstand a raid far more ferocious than those raids which had taken weaker Vilmirian towns. Elric had no idea why his countrymen had driven northwards to Bakshaan. Possibly they had come only to rest and turn their loot into food supplies in the bazaars.

The smoke of several large campfires told Elric and Moonglum where the Melnibonéans were entrenched. With a slackening of pace, they guided their horses in that direction while wet branches brushed their faces and the scents of the forest, released by the life-bringing rain, impinged sweetly upon their nostrils. It was with a feeling akin to relaxation that Elric met the outguard who suddenly appeared from the undergrowth to bar their way along the forest trail.

The Imrryrian guard was swathed in furs and steel. Beneath the visor of an intricately worked helmet he peered at Elric with wary eyes. His vision was slightly impaired by the visor and the rain which dripped from it so that he did not immediately recognize Elric.

'Halt. What do you in these parts?'

Elric said impatiently, 'Let me pass – it is Elric, your lord and your Emperor.'

The guard gasped and lowered the long-bladed spear he carried. He pushed back his helmet and gazed at the man before him with a myriad of different emotions passing across his face. Among these were amazement, reverence and hate.

He bowed stiffly. 'This is no place for you, my liege. You renounced and betrayed your people five years ago and while I acknowledge the blood of kings which flows in your veins, I cannot obey you or do you the homage which it would otherwise be your right to expect.'

20

'Of course,' said Elric proudly, sitting his horse straight-backed. 'But let your leader – my boyhood friend Dyvim Tvar – be the judge of how to deal with me. Take me to him at once and remember that my companion has done you no ill, but treat him with respect as befits the chosen friend of an Emperor of Melniboné.'

The guard bowed again and took hold of the reins of Elric's mount. He led the pair down the trail and into a large clearing wherein were pitched the tents of the men of Imrryr. Cooking fires flared in the centre of the great circle of pavilions and the fine-featured warriors of Melniboné sat talking softly around them. Even in the light of the gloomy day, the fabrics of the tents were bright and gay. The soft tones were wholly Melnibonéan in texture. Deep, smoky greens, azure, ochre, gold, dark blue. The colours did not clash – they blended. Elric felt sad nostalgia for the sundered, multi-coloured towers of Imrryr the Beautiful.

As the two companions and their guide drew nearer, men looked up in astonishment and a low muttering replaced the sounds of ordinary conversation.

'Please remain here,' the guard said to Elric. 'I will inform Lord Dyvim Tvar of your coming.' Elric nodded his acquiescence and sat firmly in his saddle conscious of the gaze of the gathered warriors. None approached him and some, whom Elric had known personally in the old days, were openly embarrassed. They were the ones who did not stare but rather averted their eyes, tending to the cooking fires or taking a sudden interest in the polish of their finely-wrought longswords and dirks. A few growled angrily, but they were in a definite minority. Most of the men were simply shocked – and also inquisitive. Why had this man, their king and their betrayer, come to their camp?

The largest pavilion, of gold and scarlet, had at its peak a banner upon which was emblazoned a dormant dragon, blue upon white. This was the tent of Dyvim Tvar and from it the Dragon Master hurried, buckling on his sword-belt,

21

his intelligent eyes puzzled and wary.

Dyvim Tvar was a man a little older than Elric and he bore the stamp of Melnibonéan nobility. His mother had been a princess, a cousin to Elric's own mother. His cheekbones were high and delicate, his eyes slightly slanting while his skull was narrow, tapering at the jaw. Like Elric, his ears were thin, near lobeless and coming almost to a point. His hands, the left one now folded around the hilt of his sword, were long-fingered and, like the rest of his skin, pale, though not nearly so pale as the dead white of the albino's. He strode towards the mounted Emperor of Melniboné and now his emotions were controlled. When he was five feet away from Elric, Dyvim Tvar bowed slowly, his head bent and his face hidden. When he looked up again, his eyes met those of Elric and remained fixed.

'Dyvim Tvar, Lord of the Dragon Caves, greets Elric, Master of Melniboné, Exponent of her Secret Arts.' The Dragon Master spoke gravely the age-old ritual greeting.

Elric was not as confident as he seemed as he replied: 'Elric, Master of Melniboné, greets his loyal subject and demands that he give audience to Dyvim Tvar.' It was not fitting, by ancient Melnibonéan standards, that the king should *request* an audience with one of his subjects and the Dragon Master understood this. He now said:

'I would be honoured if my liege would allow me to accompany him to my pavilion.'

Elric dismounted and led the way towards Dyvim Tvar's pavilion. Moonglum also dismounted and made to follow, but Elric waved him back. The two Imrryrian noblemen entered the tent.

Inside, a small oil-lamp augmented the gloomy daylight which filtered through the colourful fabric. The tent was simply furnished, possessing only a soldier's hard bed, a table and several carved wooden stools. Dyvim Tvar bowed and silently indicated one of these stools. Elric sat down.

For several moments, the two men said nothing. Neither

allowed emotion to register on their controlled features. They simply sat and stared at one another. Eventually Elric said:

'You know me for a betrayer, a thief, a murderer of my own kin and a slayer of my countrymen, Dragon Master.'

Dyvim Tvar nodded. 'With my liege's permission, I will agree with him.'

'We were never so formal in the old days, when alone,' Elric said. 'Let us forget ritual and tradition – Melniboné is broken and her sons are wanderers. We meet, as we used to, as equals – only, now, this is wholly true. We *are* equals. The Ruby Throne crashed in the ashes of Imrryr and now no emperor may sit in state.'

Dyvim Tvar sighed. 'This is true, Elric – but why have you come here? We were content to forget you. Even while thoughts of vengeance were fresh, we made no move to seek you out. Have you come to mock?'

'You know I would never do that, Dyvim Tvar. I rarely sleep, in these days, and when I do I have such dreams that I would rather be awake. You know that Yyrkoon forced me to do what I did when he usurped the throne for the second time, after I had trusted him as Regent, when, again for the second time, he put his sister, whom I loved, into a sorcerous slumber. To aid that reaver fleet was my only hope of forcing him to undo his work and release Cymoril from the spell. I was moved by vengeance but it was Stormbringer, my sword, which slew Cymoril, not I.'

'Of this, I am aware.' Dyvim Tvar sighed again and rubbed one jewelled hand across his face. 'But it does not explain why you came here. There should be no contact between you and your people. We are wary of you, Elric. Even if we allowed you to lead us again you would take your own doomed path and us with you. There is no future there for myself and my men.'

'Agreed. But I need your help for this one time – then our ways can part again.'

'We should kill you, Elric. But which would be the greater crime? Failure to do justice and slay our betrayer – or regicide? You have given me a problem at a time when there are too many problems already. Should I attempt to solve it?'

'I but played a part in history,' Elric said earnestly. 'Time would have done what I did, eventually. I but brought the day nearer – and brought it when you and our people were still resilient enough to combat it and turn to a new way of life.'

Dyvim Tvar smiled ironically. 'That is one point of view, Elric – and it has truth in it, I grant you. But tell it to the men who lost their kin and their homes because of you. Tell it to warriors who had to tend maimed comrades, to brothers, fathers and husbands whose wives, daughters and sisters – proud Melnibonéan women – were used to pleasure the barbarian pillagers.'

'Aye.' Elric dropped his eyes. When he next spoke it was quietly. 'I can do nothing to replace what our people have lost – would that I could. I yearn for Imrryr often, and her women, and her wines and entertainments. But I can offer plunder. I can offer you the richest palace in Bakshaan. Forget the old wounds and follow me this once.'

'Do you seek the riches of Bakshaan, Elric? You were never one for jewels and precious metal! Why, Elric?'

Elric ran his hands through his white hair. His red eyes were troubled. 'For vengeance, once again, Dyvim Tvar. I owe a debt to a sorcerer from Pan Tang – Theleb K'aarna. You may have heard of him – he is fairly powerful for one of a comparatively young race.'

'Then we're joined in this, Elric,' Dyvim Tvar spoke grimly. 'You are not the only Melnibonéan who owes Theleb K'aarna a debt! Because of that bitch-queen Yishana of Jharkor, one of our men was done to death a year ago in a most foul and horrible manner. Killed by Theleb K'aarna because he gave his embraces to Yishana

24

who sought a substitute for you. We can unite to avenge that blood, King Elric, and it will be a fitting excuse for those who would rather have your blood on their knives.'

Elric was not glad. He had a sudden premonition that this fortunate coincidence was to have grave and unpredictable outcomings. But he smiled.

3

In a smoking pit, somewhere beyond the limitations of
space and time, a creature stirred. All around it, shadows
moved. They were the shadows of the souls of men and
these shadows which moved through the bright darkness
were the masters of the creature. It allowed them to master
it – so long as they paid its price. In the speech of men, this
creature had a name. It was called *Quaolnargn* and would
answer to this name if called.

Now it stirred. It heard its name carrying over the
barriers which normally blocked its way to the Earth. The
calling of the name effected a temporary pathway through
those intangible barriers. It stirred again, as its name was
called for the second time. It was unaware of why it was
called or to what it was called. It was only muzzily
conscious of one fact. When the pathway was opened to it,
it could *feed*. It did not eat flesh and it did not drink blood.
It fed on the minds and the souls of adult men and women.
Occasionally, as an appetizer, it enjoyed the morsels, the
sweetmeats as it were, of the innocent life-force which it
sucked from children. It ignored animals since there was
not enough *awareness* in an animal to savour. The creature
was, for all its alien stupidity, a gourmet and a connoisseur.

Now its name was called for the third time. It stirred
again and flowed forward. The time was approaching when
it could, once again, *feed* . . .

Theleb K'aarna shuddered. He was, basically, he felt, a
man of peace. It was not his fault that his avaricious love
for Yishana had turned him mad. It was not his fault that,
because of her, he now controlled several powerful and
malevolent demons who, in return for the slaves and

enemies he fed them, protected the palace of Nikorn the merchant. He felt, very strongly, that none of it was his fault. It was circumstance which had damned him. He wished sadly that he had never met Yishana, never returned to her after that unfortunate episode outside the walls of Tanelorn. He shuddered again as he stood within the pentacle and summoned *Quaolnargn*. His embryonic talent for precognition had shown him a little of the near-future and he knew that Elric was preparing to do battle with him. Theleb K'aarna was taking the opportunity of summoning all the aid he could control. *Quaolnargn* must be sent to destroy Elric, if it could, before the albino reached the castle. Theleb K'aarna congratulated himself that he still retained the lock of white hair which had enabled him, in the past, to send another, now deceased, demon against Elric.

Quaolnargn knew that it was reaching its master. It propelled itself sluggishly forward and felt a stinging pain as it entered the alien continuum. It knew that its master's soul hovered before it but, for some reason, was disappointingly unattainable. Something was dropped in front of it. *Quaolnargn* scented at it and knew what it must do. This was part of its new *feed*. It flowed gratefully away, intent on finding its prey before the pain which was endemic of a prolonged stay in the strange place grew too much.

Elric rode at the head of his countrymen. On his right was Dyvim Tvar, the Dragon Master, on his left, Moonglum of Elwher. Behind him rode two hundred fighting men and behind them the wagons containing their loot, their war-machines and their slaves.

The caravan was resplendent with proud banners and the gleaming, long-bladed lances of Imrryr. They were clad in steel, with tapering greaves, helmets and shoulder-pieces. Their breastplates were polished and glinted where their long fur jerkins were open. Over the jerkins were flung

27

bright cloaks of Imrryrian fabrics, scintillating in the watery sunshine. The archers were immediately close to Elric and his companions. They carried unstrung bone bows of tremendous power, which only they could use. On their backs were quivers crammed with black-fletched arrows. Then came the lancers, with their shining lances at a tilt to avoid the low branches of the trees. Behind these rode the main strength – the Imrryrian swordsmen carrying longswords and shorter stabbing weapons which were too short to be real swords and too long to be named as knives. They rode, skirting Bakshaan, for the palace of Nikorn which lay to the north of Bakshaan. They rode, these men, in silence. They could think of nothing to say while Elric, their liege, led them to battle for the first time in five years.

Stormbringer, the black hellblade, tingled under Elric's hand, anticipating a new sword-quenching. Moonglum fidgeted in his saddle, nervous of the forthcoming fight which he knew would involve dark sorcery. Moonglum had no liking for the sorcerous arts or for the creatures they spawned. To his mind, men should fight their own battles without help. They rode on, nervous and tense.

Stormbringer shook against Elric's side. A faint moan emanated from the metal and the tone was one of warning. Elric raised a hand and the cavalcade reined to a halt.

'There is something coming near which only I can deal with,' he informed the men. 'I will ride on ahead.'

He spurred his horse into a wary canter, keeping his eyes before him. Stormbringer's voice was louder, sharper – a muted shriek. The horse trembled and Elric's own nerves were tense. He had not expected trouble so soon and he prayed that whatever evil was lurking in the forest was not directed against him.

'Arioch, be with me,' he breathed. 'Aid me now, and I'll dedicate a score of warriors to you. Aid me, Arioch.'

A foul odour forced itself into Elric's nostrils. He coughed and covered his mouth with his hands, his eyes seeking the source of the stink. The horse whinnied. Elric jumped from the saddle and slapped his mount on the rump, sending it back along the trail. He crouched warily, Stormbringer now in his grasp, the black metal quivering from point to pommel.

He sensed it with the witch-sight of his forefathers before he saw it with his eyes. And he recognized its shape. He, himself, was one of its masters. But this time he had no control over *Quaolnargn* – he was standing in no pentacle and his only protection was his blade and his wits. He knew, also, of the power of *Quaolnargn* and shuddered. Could he overcome such a horror singlehandedly?

'*Arioch! Arioch! Aid me!*' It was a scream, high and desperate.

'*Arioch!*'

There was no time to conjure a spell. *Quaolnargn* was before him, a great green toad-thing which hopped along the trail obscenely, moaning to itself in its Earth-fostered pain. It towered over Elric so that the albino was in its shadow before it was ten feet away from him. Elric breathed quickly and screamed once more: '*Arioch! Blood and souls, if you aid me, now!*'

Suddenly, the toad-demon leapt.

Elric sprang to one side, but was caught by a long-nailed foot which sent him flying into the undergrowth. *Quaolnargn* turned clumsily and its filthy mouth opened hungrily, displaying a deep toothless cavity from which a foul odour poured.

'*Arioch!*'

In its evil and alien insensitivity, the toad-thing did not even recognize the name of so powerful a demon-god. It could not be frightened – it had to be fought.

And as it approached Elric for the second time, the clouds belched rain from their bowels and a downpour lashed the forest.

Half-blinded by the rain smashing against his face, Elric

29

backed behind a tree, his runesword ready. In ordinary terms, *Quaolnargn* was blind. It could not see Elric or the forest. It could not feel the rain. It could only see and smell men's souls – its *feed*. The toad-demon blundered past him and, as it did so, Elric leapt high, holding his blade with both hands, and plunged it to the hilt into the demon's soft and quivering back. Flesh – or whatever Earth-bound stuff formed the demon's body – squelched nauseatingly. Elric pulled at Stormbringer's hilt as the sorcerous sword seared into the hellbeast's back, cutting down where the spine should be but where no spine was. *Quaolnargn* piped its pain. Its voice was thin and reedy, even in such extreme agony. It retaliated.

Elric felt his mind go numb and then his head was filled with a pain which was not natural in any sense. He could not even shriek. His eyes widened in horror as he realized what was happening to him. His soul was being drawn from his body. He knew it. He felt no physical weakness, he was only aware of looking out into . . .

But even that awareness was fading. Everything was fading, even the pain, even the dreadful hell-spawned pain.

'Arioch!' he croaked.

Savagely, he summoned strength from somewhere. Not from himself, not even from Stormbringer – from somewhere. Something was aiding him at last, giving him strength – enough strength to do what he must.

He wrenched the blade from the demon's back. He stood over *Quaolnargn*. Above him. He was floating somewhere, not in the air of Earth. Just floating over the demon. With thoughtful deliberation he selected a spot on the demon's skull which he somehow knew to be the only spot on his body where Stormbringer might slay. Slowly and carefully, he lowered Stormbringer and twisted the runesword through *Quaolnargn*'s skull.

The toad-thing whimpered, dropped – and vanished.

Elric lay sprawled in the undergrowth, trembling the

length of his aching body. He picked himself up slowly. All his energy had been drained from him. Stormbringer, too, seemed to have lost its vitality, but that, Elric knew would return and, in returning, bring him new strength.

But then he felt his whole frame tugged rigid. He was astounded. What was happening? His senses began to blank out. He had the feeling that he was staring down a long, black tunnel which stretched into nowhere. Everything was vague. He was aware of motion. He was travelling. How – or where, he could not tell.

For brief seconds he travelled, conscious only of an unearthly feeling of motion and the fact that Stormbringer, his life, was clutched in his right hand.

Then he felt hard stone beneath him and he opened his eyes – or was it, he wondered, that his vision returned? – and looked up at the gloating face above him.

'Theleb K'aarna,' he whispered hoarsely, 'how did you effect this?'

The sorcerer bent down and tugged Stormbringer from Elric's enfeebled grasp. He sneered. 'I followed your commendable battle with my messenger, Lord Elric. When it was obvious that somehow you had summoned aid – I quickly conjured another spell and brought you here. Now I have your sword and your strength. I know that without it you are nothing. You are in my power, Elric of Melniboné.'

Elric gasped air into his lungs. His whole body was pain-racked. He tried to smile, but he could not. It was not in his nature to smile when he was beaten. 'Give me back my sword.'

Theleb K'aarna gave a self-satisfied smirk. He chuckled. 'Who talks of vengeance, now, Elric?'

'Give me my sword!' Elric tried to rise but he was too weak. His vision blurred until he could hardly see the gloating sorcerer.

'And what kind of bargain do you offer?' Theleb K'aarna asked. 'You are not a well man, Lord Elric – and sick men

31

do not bargain. They beg.'

Elric trembled in impotent anger. He tightened his mouth. He would not beg – neither would he bargain. In silence, he glowered at the sorcerer.

'I think that first,' Theleb K'aarna said smiling. 'I shall lock this away.' He hefted Stormbringer in his hand and turned towards a cupboard behind him. From his robes he produced a key with which he unlocked the cupboard and placed the runesword inside, carefully locking the door again when he had done so. 'Then, I think, I'll show our virile hero to his ex-mistress – the sister of the man he betrayed four years ago.'

Elric said nothing.

'After that,' Theleb K'aarna continued, 'my employer Nikorn shall be shown the assassin who thought he could do what others failed to achieve.' He smiled. 'What a day,' he chuckled. 'What a day! So full. So rich with pleasure.'

Theleb K'aarna tittered and picked up a hand-bell. He rang it. A door behind Elric opened and two tall desert warriors strode in. They glanced at Elric and then at Theleb K'aarna. They were evidently amazed.

'No questions,' Theleb K'aarna snapped. 'Take this refuse to the chambers of Queen Yishana.'

Elric fumed as he was hefted up between the two. The men were dark-skinned, bearded and their eyes were deep-set beneath shaggy brows. They wore the heavy wool-trimmed metal caps of their race, and their armour was not of iron but of thick, leather-covered wood. Down a long corridor they lugged Elric's weakened body and one of them rapped sharply on a door.

Elric recognized Yishana's voice bid them enter. Behind the desertmen and their burden came the tittering, fussing sorcerer. 'A present for you, Yishana,' he called.

The desertmen entered. Elric could not see Yishana but he heard her gasp. 'On the couch,' directed the sorcerer. Elric was deposited on yielding fabric. He lay completely exhausted on the couch, staring up at a bright, lewd mural which had been painted on the ceiling.

Yishana bent over him. Elric could smell her erotic perfume. He said hoarsely: 'An unprecedented reunion, Queen.' Yishana's eyes were, for a moment, concerned, then they hardened and she laughed cynically.

'Oh – my hero has returned to me at last. But I'd rather he'd come at his own volition, not dragged here by the back of his neck like a puppy. The wolf's teeth have all been drawn and there's no one to savage me at nights.' She turned away, disgust on her painted face. 'Take him away, Theleb K'aarna. You have proved your point.'

The sorcerer nodded.

'And now,' he said, 'to visit Nikorn – I think he should be expecting us by this time . . .'

4

Nikorn of Ilmar was not a young man. He was well past fifty but had preserved his youth. His face was that of a peasant, firm-boned but not fleshy. His eyes were keen and hard as he stared at Elric who had been mockingly propped in a chair.

'So you are Elric of Melniboné, the Wolf of the Snarling Sea, spoiler, reaver and woman-slayer. I think that you could hardly slay a child now. However, I will say that it discomforts me to see any man in such a position – particularly one who has been so active as you. Is it true what the spell-maker says? Were you sent here by my enemies to assassinate me?'

Elric was concerned for his men. What would they do? Wait – or go on. If they stormed the palace now they were doomed – and so was he.

'Is it true?' Nikorn was insistent.

'No,' whispered Elric. 'My quarrel was with Theleb K'aarna. I have an old score to settle with him.'

'I am not interested in old scores, my friend,' Nikorn said, not unkindly. 'I *am* interested in preserving my life. Who sent you here?'

'Theleb K'aarna speaks falsely if he told you I was sent,' Elric lied. 'I was interested only in paying my debt.'

'It is not only the sorcerer who told me, I'm afraid,' Nikorn said. 'I have many spies in the city and two of them independently informed me of a plot by local merchants to employ you to kill me.'

Elric smiled faintly. 'Very well,' he agreed. 'It was true, but I had no intention of doing what they asked.'

Nikorn said: 'I might believe you, Elric of Melniboné. But now I do not know what to do with you. I would not

34

turn anyone over to Theleb K'aarna's mercies. May I have your word that you will not make an attempt on my life again?'

'Are we bargaining, Master Nikorn?' Elric said faintly.

'We are.'

'Then what do I give my word in return for, sir?'

'Your life and freedom, Lord Elric.'

'And my sword?'

Nikorn shrugged regretfully. 'I'm sorry – not your sword.'

'Then take my life,' said Elric brokenly.

'Come now – my bargain's good. Have your life and freedom and give your word that you will not plague me again.'

Elric breathed deeply. 'Very well.'

Nikorn moved away. Theleb K'aarna who had been standing in the shadows put a hand on the merchant's arm. 'You're going to release him?'

'Aye,' Nikorn said. 'He's no threat to either of us now.'

Elric was aware of a certain feeling of friendship in Nikorn's attitude towards him. He, too, felt something of the same. Here was a man both courageous and clever. But – Elric fought madness – without Stormbringer, what could he do to fight back?

The two hundred Imrryrian warriors lay hidden in the undergrowth as dusk gave way to night. They watched and wondered. What had happened to Elric? Was he now in the castle as Dyvim Tvar thought? The Dragon Master knew something of the art of divining, as did all members of the royal line of Melniboné. From what small spells he had conjured, it seemed that Elric now lay within the castle walls.

But without Elric to battle Theleb K'aarna's power, how could they take it?

Nikorn's palace was also a fortress, bleak and unlovely.

It was surrounded by a deep moat of dark, stagnant water. It stood high above the surrounding forest, built into rather than on to the rock. Much of it had been carved out of the living stone. It was sprawling and rambling and covered a large area, surrounded by natural buttresses. The rock was porous in places, and slimy water ran down the walls of the lower parts, spreading through dark moss. It was not a pleasant place, judging from the outside, but it was almost certainly impregnable. Two hundred men could not take it, without the aid of magic.

Some of the Melnibonéan warriors were becoming impatient. There were a few who muttered that Elric had, once again, betrayed them. Dyvim Tvar and Moonglum did not believe this. They had seen the signs of conflict – and heard them – in the forest.

They waited: Hoping for a signal from the castle itself.

They watched the castle's great main gate – and their patience at last proved of value. The huge wood and metal gate swung inwards on chains and a white-faced man in the tattered regalia of Melniboné appeared between two desert warriors. They were supporting him, it seemed. They pushed him forward – he staggered a few yards along the causeway of slimy stone which bridged the moat.

Then he fell. He began to crawl wearily, painfully, forward.

Moonglum growled. 'What have they done to him? I must help him.' But Dyvim Tvar held him back.

'No – it would not do to betray our presence here. Let him reach the forest first, then we can help him.'

Even those who had cursed Elric, now felt pity for the albino as, staggering and crawling alternately, he dragged his body slowly towards them. From the battlements of the fortress a tittering laugh was borne down to the ears of those below. They also caught a few words.

'*What now, wolf?*' said the voice. '*What now?*'

Moonglum clenched his hands and trembled with rage,

hating to see his proud friend so mocked in his weakness. 'What's happened to him? What have they done?'

'Patience,' Dyvim Tvar said. 'We'll find out in a short while.'

It was an agony to wait until Elric finally crawled on his knees into the undergrowth.

Moonglum went forward to aid his friend. He put a supporting arm around Elric's shoulders but the albino snarled and shook it off, his whole countenance aflame with terrible hate – made more terrible because it was impotent. Elric could do nothing to destroy that which he hated. Nothing.

Dyvim Tvar said urgently: 'Elric, you must tell us what happened. If we're to help you – we must know what happened.'

Elric breathed heavily and nodded his agreement. His face partially cleared of the emotion he felt and weakly he stuttered out the story.

'So,' Moonglum growled, 'our plans come to nothing – and you have lost your strength for ever.'

Elric shook his head. 'There must be a way,' he gasped. 'There must!'

'What? How? If you have a plan, Elric – let me hear it now.'

Elric swallowed thickly and mumbled. 'Very well, Moonglum, you shall hear it. But listen carefully, for I have not the strength to repeat it.'

Moonglum was a lover of the night, but only when it was lit by the torches found in cities. He did not like the night when it came to open countryside and he was not fond of it when it surrounded a castle such as Nikorn's, but he pressed on and hoped for the best.

If Elric had been right in his interpretation, then the battle might yet be won and Nikorn's palace taken. But it still meant danger for Moonglum and he was not one deliberately to put himself into danger.

As he viewed the stagnant waters of the moat with distaste he reflected that this was enough to test any friendship to the utmost. Philosophically, he lowered himself down into the water and began to swim across it.

The moss on the fortress offered a flimsy handhold, but it led to ivy which gave a better grip. Moonglum slowly clambered up the wall. He hoped that Elric had been right and that Theleb K'aarna would need to rest for a while before he could work more sorcery. That was why Elric had suggested he make haste. Moonglum clambered on, and eventually reached the small unbarred window he sought. A normal size man could not have entered, but Moonglum's small frame was proving useful.

He wriggled through the gap, shivering with cold, and landed on the hard stone of a narrow staircase which ran both up and down the interior wall of the fortress. Moonglum frowned, and then took the steps leading upwards. Elric had given him a rough idea of how to reach his destination.

Expecting the worst, he went soft-footed up the stone steps. He went towards the chambers of Yishana, Queen of Jharkor.

In an hour, Moonglum was back, shivering with cold and dripping with water. In his hands he carried Stormbringer. He carried the runesword with cautious care – nervous of its sentient evil. It was alive again; alive with black, pulsating life.

'Thank the gods I was right,' Elric murmured weakly from where he lay surrounded by two or three Imrryrians, including Dyvim Tvar who was staring at the albino with concern. 'I prayed that I was correct in my assumption and Theleb K'aarna was resting after his earlier exertions on my behalf . . .'

He stirred, and Dyvim Tvar helped him to sit upright.

38

Elric reached out a long white hand – reached like an addict of some terrible drug towards the sword. 'Did you give her my message?' he asked as he gratefully seized the pommel.

'Aye,' Moonglum said shakily, 'and she agreed. You were also right in your other interpretation, Elric. It did not take her long to inveigle the key out of a weary Theleb K'aarna. The sorcerer was tremendously tired and Nikorn was becoming nervous wondering if an attack of any kind would take place while Theleb K'aarna was incapable of action. She went herself to the cupboard and got me the blade.'

'Women can sometimes be useful,' said Dyvim Tvar dryly. 'Though usually, in matters like these, they're a hindrance.' It was possible to see that something other than immediate problems of taking the castle were worrying Dyvim Tvar, but no one thought to ask him what it was that bothered him. It seemed a personal thing.

'I agree, Dragon Master,' Elric said, almost gaily. The gathered men were aware of the strength which poured swiftly back into the albino's deficient veins, imbuing him with a new hellborn vitality. 'It is time for our vengeance. But remember – no harm to Nikorn. I gave him my word.'

He folded his right hand firmly around Stormbringer's hilt. 'Now for a sword-quenching. I believe I can obtain the help of just the allies we need to keep the sorcerer occupied while we storm the castle. I'll need no pentacle to summon my friends of the air!'

Moonglum licked his long lips. 'So it's sorcery again. In truth, Elric, this whole country is beginning to stink of wizardry and the minions of Hell.'

Elric murmured for his friend's ears: 'No Hell-beings these – but honest elementals, equally powerful in many ways. Curb your belly-fear, Moonglum – a little more simple conjuring and Theleb K'aarna will have no desire to retaliate.'

The albino frowned, remembering the secret pacts of his

forefathers. He took a deep breath and closed his pain-filled scarlet eyes. He swayed, the runesword half-loose in his grip. His chant was low, like the far-off moaning of the wind itself. His chest moved quickly up and down, and some of the younger warriors, those who had never been fully initiated into the ancient lore of Melniboné, stirred with discomfort. Elric's voice was not addressing human folk – his words were for the invisible, the intangible – the supernatural. An old and ancient rhyme began the casting of word-runes . . .

'Hear, the doomed one's dark decision,
Let the Wind Giant's wail be heard,
Graoll and Misha's mighty moaning
Send my enemy like a bird.

'By the sultry scarlet stones,
By the bane of my black blade,
By the Lasshaar's lonely mewling,
Let a mighty wind be made.

'Speed of sunbeams from their homeland,
Swifter than the sundering storm,
Speed of arrow deerwards shooting,
Let the sorcerer so be borne.'

His voice broke and he called high and clear:
'Misha! Misha! In the name of my fathers I summon thee, Lord of the Winds!'
Almost at once, the trees of the forest suddenly bent as if some great hand had brushed them aside. A terrible soughing voice swam from nowhere. And all but Elric, deep in his trance, shivered.

'ELRIC OF MELNIBONÉ,' the voice roared like a distant storm, 'WE KNEW YOUR FATHERS. I KNOW THEE. THE DEBT WE OWE THE LINE OF ELRIC IS FORGOTTEN BY MORTALS

BUT GRAOLL AND MISHA, KINGS OF THE WIND, REMEMBER.
HOW MAY THE LASSHAAR AID THEE?'

The voice seemed almost friendly – but proud and aloof and
awe-inspiring.

Elric, completely in a state of trance now, jerked his whole
body in convulsions. His voice shrieked piercingly from his
throat – and the words were alien, unhuman, violently
disturbing to the ears and nerves of the human listeners. Elric
spoke briefly and then the invisible Wind Giant's great voice
roared and sighed:

'I WILL DO AS YOU DESIRE.' Then the trees bent once more
and the forest was still and muted.

Somewhere in the gathered ranks, a man sneezed sharply
and this was a sign for others to start talking – speculating.

For many moments, Elric remained in his trance and then,
quite suddenly, he opened his enigmatic eyes and looked
gravely around him, puzzled for a second. Then he clasped
Stormbringer more firmly and leaned forward, speaking to
the men of Imrryr. 'Soon Theleb K'aarna will be in our power,
my friends, and so also will we possess the loot of Nikorn's
palace!'

But Dyvim Tvar shuddered then. 'I'm not so given skilled in
the esoteric arts as you, Elric,' he said quietly. 'But in my soul I
see three wolves leading a pack to slaughter and one of those
wolves must die. My doom is near me, I think.'

Elric said uncomfortably: 'Worry not, Dragon Master.
You'll live to mock the ravens and spend the spoils of
Bakshaan.' But his voice was not convincing.

5

In his bed of silk and ermine, Theleb K'aarna stirred and awoke. He had a brooding inkling of coming trouble and he remembered that earlier in his tiredness he had given more to Yishana than had been wise. He could not remember what it was and now he had a presentiment of danger – the closeness of which over-shadowed thoughts of any past indiscretion. He arose hurriedly and pulled his robe over his head, shrugging into it as he walked towards a strangely-silvered mirror which was set on one wall of his chamber and reflected no image.

With bleary eyes and trembling hands he began preparations. From one of the many earthenware jars resting on a bench near the window, he poured a substance which seemed like dried blood mottled with the hardened blue venom of the black serpent whose homeland was in far Dorel which lay on the edge of the world. Over this, he muttered a swift incantation, scooped the stuff into a crucible and hurled it at the mirror, one arm shielding his eyes. A crack sounded, hard and sharp to his ears, and bright green light erupted suddenly and was gone. The mirror flickered deep within itself, the silvering seemed to undulate and flicker and flash and then a picture began to form.

Theleb K'aarna knew that the sight he witnessed had taken place in the recent past. It showed him Elric's summoning of the Wind Giants.

Theleb K'aarna's dark features grinned with a terrible fear. His hands jerked as spasms shook him. Half-gibbering, he rushed back to his bench and, leaning his hands upon it, stared out of the window into the deep night. He knew what to expect.

42

A great and dreadful storm was blowing – and he was the object of the Lasshaar's attack. He *had* to retaliate, else his own soul would be wrenched from him by the Giants of the Wind and flung to the air spirits, to be borne for eternity on the winds of the world. Then his voice would moan like a banshee around the cold peaks of high ice-clothed mountains for ever – lost and lonely. His soul would be damned to travel with the four winds wherever their caprice might bear it, knowing no rest.

Theleb K'aarna had a respect born of fear for the powers of the aeromancer, the rare wizard who could control the wind elementals – and aeromancy was only one of the arts which Elric and his ancestors possessed. Then Theleb K'aarna realized what he was battling – ten thousand years and hundreds of generations of sorcerers who had gleaned knowledge from the Earth and beyond it and passed it down to the albino whom he, Theleb K'aarna, had sought to destroy. Then Theleb K'aarna fully regretted his actions. Then – it was too late.

The sorcerer had no control over the powerful Wind Giants as Elric had. His only hope was to combat one element with another. The fire-spirits must be summoned, and quickly. All of Theleb K'aarna's pyromantic powers would be required to hold off the ravening supernatural winds which were soon to shake the air and the earth. Even Hell would shake to the sound and the thunder of the Wind Giants' wrath.

Quickly, Theleb K'aarna marshalled his thoughts and, with trembling hands, began to make strange passes in the air and promise unhealthy pacts with whichever of the powerful fire elementals would help him this once. He promised himself to eternal death for the sake of a few more years of life.

With the gathering of the Wind Giants came the thunder and the rain. The lightning flashed sporadically, but not lethally. It never touched the Earth. Elric, Moonglum and the men of Imrryr were aware of disturbing movements in the atmosphere, but only Elric with his witch sight could see a little of what was happening. The Lasshaar Giants were invisible to other eyes.

The war engines which the Imrryians were even now constructing from pre-fashioned parts were puny things compared to the Wind Giants' might. But victory depended upon these engines since the Lasshaar's fight would be with the supernatural not the natural.

Battle-rams and siege ladders were slowly taking shape as the warriors worked with frantic speed. The hour of the storming came closer as the wind rose and thunder rattled. The moon was blanked out by huge billowings of black cloud, and the men worked by the light of torches. Surprise was no great asset in an attack of the kind planned.

Two hours before dawn, they were ready.

At last the men of Imrryr, Elric, Dyvim Tvar and Moonglum riding high at their head, moved towards the castle of Nikorn. As they did so, Elric raised his voice in an unholy shout – and thunder rumbled in answer to him. A great gout of lightning seared out of the sky towards the palace and the whole place shook and trembled as a ball of mauve and orange fire suddenly appeared over the castle and *absorbed* the lightning! The battle between fire and air had begun.

The surrounding countryside was alive with a weird and malignant shrieking and moaning, deafening to the ears of the marching men. They sensed conflict all round them, and only a little was visible.

Over most of the castle an unearthly glow hung, waxing and waning, defending a gibbering wretch of a sorcerer who knew that he was doomed if once the Lords of the Flame gave way to the roaring Wind Giants.

Elric smiled without humour as he observed the war. On the supernatural plane, he now had little to fear. But there was still the castle and he had no extra supernatural aid to help him take that. Swordplay and skill in battle was the only hope against the ferocious desert warriors who now crowded the battlements, preparing to destroy the two hundred men who came against them.

Up rose the Dragon Standards their cloth-of-gold fabric flashing in the eerie glow. Spread out, walking slowly, the sons of Imrryr moved forward to do battle. Up, also, rose the siege ladders as captains directed warriors to begin the assault. The defenders' faces were pale spots against the dark stone and thin shouts came from them; but it was impossible to catch their words.

Two great battle-rams, fashioned the day before, were brought to the vanguard of the approaching warriors. The narrow causeway was a dangerous one to pass over, but it was the only means of crossing the moat at ground level. Twenty men carried each of the great iron-tipped rams and now they began to run forward while arrows hailed downwards. Their shields protecting them from most of the shafts, the warriors reached the causeway and rushed across it. Now the first ram connected with the gate. It seemed to Elric as he watched this operation that nothing of wood and iron could withstand the vicious impact of the ram, but the gates shivered almost imperceptibly – and held!

Like vampires, hungry for blood, the men howled and staggered aside crabwise to let pass the log held by their comrades. Again the gates shivered, more easily noticed this time, but they yet held.

Dyvim Tvar roared encouragement to those now scaling the siege ladders. These were brave, almost desperate men, for few of the first climbers would reach the top and even if they were successful, they would be hard-pressed to stay alive until their comrades arrived.

Boiling lead hissed from great cauldrons set on spindles so that they could be easily emptied and filled quickly.

Many a brave Imrryrian warrior fell earthwards, dead from the searing metal before he reached the sharp rocks beneath. Large stones were released out of leather bags hanging from rotating pulleys which could swing out beyond the battlements and rain bone-crushing death on the besiegers. But still the invaders advanced, voicing half-a-hundred war-shouts and steadily scaling their long ladders, whilst their comrades, using a shield barrier still, to protect their heads, concentrated on breaking down the gates.

Elric and his two companions could do little to help the scalers or the rammers at that stage. All three were hand-to-hand fighters, leaving even the archery to their rear ranks of bowmen who stood in rows and shot their shafts high into the castle defenders.

The gates were beginning to give. Cracks and splits appeared in them, ever widening. Then, all at once, when hardly expected, the right gate creaked on tortured hinges and fell. A triumphant roar erupted from the throats of the invaders and, dropping their hold on the logs, they led their companions through the breach, axes and maces swinging like scythes and flails before them – and enemy heads springing from necks like wheat from the stalk.

'The castle is ours!' shouted Moonglum, running forward and upward towards the gap in the archway. 'The castle's taken.'

'Speak not too hastily of victory,' replied Dyvim Tvar, but he laughed as he spoke and ran as fast as the others to reach the castle.

'And where is your doom, now?' Elric called to his fellow Melnibonéan, then broke off sharply when Dyvim Tvar's face clouded and his mouth set grimly. For a moment there was tension between them, even as they ran, then Dyvim Tvar laughed loud and made a joke of it. 'It lies somewhere, Elric, it lies somewhere – but let us not worry about such things, for if my doom hangs over me, I cannot stop its

46

descent when my hour arrives!' He slapped Elric's shoulder, feeling for the albino's uncharacteristic confusion.

Then they were under the mighty archway and in the courtyard of the castle where savage fighting had developed almost into single duels, enemy choosing enemy and fighting him to the death.

Stormbringer was the first of the three men's blades to take blood and send a desertman's soul to Hell. The song it sang as it was lashed through the air in strong strokes was an evil one – evil and triumphant.

The dark-faced desert warriors were famous for their courage and skill with swords. Their curved blades were reaping havoc in the Imrryrian ranks for, at that stage, the desertmen far outnumbered the Melnibonéan force.

Somewhere above, the inspired scalers had got a firm foothold on the battlements and were closing with the men of Nikorn, driving them back, forcing many over the unrailed edges of the parapets. A falling, still screaming warrior plummeted down, to land almost on Elric, knocking his shoulder and causing him to fall heavily to the blood-and-rain-slick cobbles. A badly scarred desertman, quick to see his chance, moved forward with a gloating look on his travesty of a face. His scimitar moved up, poised to hack Elric's neck from his shoulders, and then his helmet split open and his forehead spurted a sudden gout of blood.

Dyvim Tvar wrenched a captured axe from the skull of the slain warrior and grinned at Elric as the albino rose.

'We'll both live to see victory, yet,' he shouted over the din of the warring elementals above them and the sound of clashing arms. 'My doom, I will escape until –' He broke off, a look of surprise on his fine-boned face, and Elric's stomach twisted inside him as he saw a steel point appear in Dyvim Tvar's right side. Behind the Dragon Master, a maliciously smiling desert warrior pulled his blade from Dyvim Tvar's body. Elric cursed and rushed forward. The man put up his blade to defend himself, backing hurriedly

47

away from the infuriated albino. Stormbringer swung up and then down, it howled a death-song and sheared right through the curved steel of Elric's opponent – and it kept on going, straight through the man's shoulder blade, splitting him half in two. Elric turned back to Dyvim Tvar who was still standing up, but was pale and strained. His blood dripped from his wound and seeped through his garments.

'How badly are you hurt?' Elric said anxiously. 'Can you tell?'

'That trollspawn's sword passed through my ribs, I think – no vitals were harmed.' Dyvim Tvar gasped and tried to smile. 'I'm sure I'd know if he'd made more of the wound.'

Then he fell. And when Elric turned him, he looked into a dead and staring face. The Dragon Master, Lord of the Dragon Caves, would never tend his beasts again.

Elric felt sick and weary as he got up, standing over the body of his kinsman. Because of me, he thought, another fine man has died. But this was the only conscious thought he allowed himself for the meantime. He was forced to defend himself from the slashing swords of a couple of desertmen who came at him in a rush.

The archers, their work done outside, came running through the breach in the gate and their arrows poured into the enemy ranks.

Elric shouted loudly: 'My kinsman Dyvim Tvar lies dead, stabbed in the back by a desert warrior – avenge him, brethren. Avenge the Dragon Master of Imrryr!'

A low moaning came from the throats of the Melnibonéans and their attack was even more ferocious than before. Elric called to a bunch of axe-men who ran down from the battlements, their victory assured.

'You men, follow me. We can avenge the blood that Theleb K'aarna took!' He had a good idea of the geography of the castle.

Moonglum shouted from somewhere. 'One moment, Elric, and I'll join you!' A desert warrior fell, his back to Elric, and from behind him emerged a grinning Moonglum, his sword covered in blood from point to pommel.

Elric led the way to a small door, set into the main tower of the castle. He pointed at it and spoke to the axe-men. 'Set to with your axes, lads, and hurry!'

Grimly, the axe-men began to hack at the tough timber. Impatiently, Elric watched as the wood chips started to fly.

The conflict was appalling. Theleb K'aarna sobbed in frustration. Kakatal, the Fire Lord, and his minions were having little effect on the Wind Giants. Their power appeared to be increasing if anything. The sorcerer gnawed his knuckles and quaked in his chamber while below him the human warriors fought, bled and died. Theleb K'aarna made himself concentrate on one thing only – total destruction of the Lasshaar forces. But he knew, somehow, even then, that sooner or later, in one way or another, he was doomed.

The axes drove deeper and deeper into the stout timber. At last it gave. 'We're through, my lord.' One of the axe-men indicated the gaping hole they'd made.

Elric reached his arm through the gap and prised up the bar which secured the door. The bar moved upwards and then fell with a clatter to the stone flagging. Elric put his shoulder to the door and pushed.

Above them, now, two huge, almost-human figures had appeared in the sky, outlined against the night. One was golden and glowing like the sun and seemed to wield a great sword of fire. The other was dark blue and silver, writhing, smoke-like, with a flickering spear of restless orange in his hand.

Misha and Kakatal clashed. The outcome of their mighty struggle might well decide Theleb K'aarna's fate.

'Quickly,' Elric said. 'Upwards!'

They ran up the stairs. The stairs which led to Theleb K'aarna's chamber.

Suddenly the men were forced to stop as they came to a door of jet-black, studded with crimson iron. It had no keyhole, no bolts, no bars, but it was quite secure. Elric directed the axe-men to begin hewing at it. All six struck at the door in unison.

In unison, they screamed and vanished. Not even a wisp of smoke remained to mark where they had disappeared.

Moonglum staggered backwards, eyes wide in fear. He was backing away from Elric who remained firmly by the door, Stormbringer throbbing in his hand. 'Get out, Elric – this is a sorcery of terrible power. Let your friends of the air finish the wizard!'

Elric shouted half-hysterically: 'Magic is best fought by magic!' He hurled his whole body behind the blow which he struck at the black door. Stormbringer whined into it, shrieked as if in victory and howled like a soul-hungry demon. There was a blinding flash, a roaring in Elric's ears, a sense of weightlessness; and then the door had crashed inwards. Moonglum witnessed this – he had remained against his will.

'Stormbringer has rarely failed me, Moonglum,' cried Elric as he leapt through the aperture. 'Come, we have reached Theleb K'aarna's den—' He broke off, staring at the gibbering thing on the floor. It had been a man. It had been Theleb K'aarna. Now it was hunched and twisted – sitting in the middle of a broken pentacle and tittering to itself.

Suddenly, intelligence came into its eyes. 'Too late for vengeance, Lord Elric,' it said. 'I have won, you see – I have claimed your vengeance as my own.'

Grim-faced and speechless, Elric stepped forward, lifted Stormbringer and brought the moaning runesword down into the sorcerer's skull. He left it there for several moments.

'Drink your fill, hell-blade,' he murmured. 'We have earned it, you and I.'

Overhead, there was a sudden silence.

6

'It's untrue! You lie!' screamed the frightened man. 'We
were not responsible.' Pilarmo faced the group of leading
citizens. Behind the overdressed merchant were his three
colleagues – those who had earlier met Elric and Moonglum in the tavern.

One of the accusing citizens pointed a chubby finger
towards the north and Nikorn's palace.

'So – Nikorn was an enemy of all other traders in
Bakshaan. That I accept. But now a horde of bloody-
handed reavers attack his castle with the aid of demons –
and Elric of Melniboné leads them! You know that you
were responsible – the gossip's all over the city. You
employed Elric – and this is what's happened!'

'But we didn't know he would go to such lengths to kill
Nikorn!' Fat Tormiel wrung his hands, his face aggrieved
and afraid. 'You are wronging us. We only . . .'

'We're wronging *you*!' Faratt, spokesman for his fellow
citizens, was thick-lipped and florid. He waved his hands in
angry exasperation. 'When Elric and his jackals have done
with Nikorn – they'll come to the city. Fool! That is what
the albino sorcerer planned to begin with. He was only
mocking you – for you provided him with an excuse.
Armed men we can fight – but not foul sorcery!'

'What shall we do? What shall we do? Bakshaan will be
razed within the day!' Tormiel turned on Pilarmo. 'This
was your idea – you think of a plan!'

Pilarmo stuttered: 'We could pay a ransom – bribe them
– give them enough money to satisfy them.'

'And who shall give this money?' asked Faratt.

Again the argument began.

*　　*　　*

Elric looked with distaste at Theleb K'aarna's broken corpse. He turned away and faced a blanch-featured Moonglum who said hoarsely: 'Let's away, now, Elric. Yishana awaits you in Bakshaan as she promised. You must keep your end of the bargain I made for you.'

Elric nodded wearily. 'Aye – the Imrryrians seem to have taken the castle by the sound of it. We'll leave them to their spoiling and get out while we may. Will you allow me a few moments here, alone? The sword rejects the soul.'

Moonglum sighed thankfully. 'I'll join you in the courtyard within the quarter hour. I wish to claim some measure of the spoils.' He left clattering down the stairs while Elric remained standing over his enemy's body. He spread out his arms, the sword, dripping blood, still in his hand.

'Dyvim Tvar,' he cried. 'You and our countrymen have been avenged. Let any evil one who holds the soul of Dyvim Tvar release it now and take instead the soul of Theleb K'aarna.'

Within the room something invisible and intangible – but sensed all the same – flowed and hovered over the sprawled body of Theleb K'aarna. Elric looked out of the window and thought he heard the beating of dragon wings – smelled the acrid breath of dragons – saw a shape winging across the dawn sky bearing Dyvim Tvar the Dragon Master away.

Elric half-smiled. 'The Gods of Melniboné protect thee wherever thou art,' he said quietly and turned away from the carnage, leaving the room.

On the stairway, he met Nikorn of Ilmar.

The merchant's rugged face was full of anger. He trembled with rage. There was a big sword in his hand.

'So I've found you, wolf,' he said. 'I gave you your life – and you have done this to me!'

Elric said tiredly: 'It was to be. But I gave my word that I would not take your life and, believe me, I would not,

53

Nikorn, even had I not pledged my word.'

Nikorn stood two steps from the door blocking the exit 'Then I'll take yours. Come – engage!' He moved out into the courtyard, half-stumbled over an Imrryrian corpse, righted himself and waited, glowering, for Elric to emerge. Elric did so, his runesword sheathed.

'No.'

'Defend yourself, wolf!'

Automatically, the albino's right hand crossed to his sword hilt, but he still did not unsheath it. Nikorn cursed and aimed a well-timed blow which barely missed the white-faced sorcerer. He skipped back and now he tugged out Stormbringer, still reluctant, and stood poised and wary, waiting for the Bakshaanite's next move.

Elric intended simply to disarm Nikorn. He did not want to kill or maim this brave man who had spared him when he had been entirely at the other's mercy.

Nikorn swung another powerful stroke at Elric and the albino parried. Stormbringer was moaning softly, shuddering and pulsating. Metal clanged and then the fight was on in full earnest as Nikorn's rage turned to calm, possessed fury. Elric was forced to defend himself with all his skill and power. Though older than the albino, and a city merchant, Nikorn was a superb swordsman. His speed was fantastic and, at times, Elric was not on the defensive only because he desired it.

But something was happening to the runeblade. It was twisting in Elric's hand and forcing him to make a counterattack. Nikorn backed away – a light akin to fear in his eyes as he realized the potency of Elric's hell-forged steel. The merchant fought grimly – and Elric did not fight at all. He felt entirely in the power of the whining sword which hacked and cut at Nikorn's guard.

Stormbringer suddenly shifted in Elric's hand. Nikorn screamed. The runesword left Elric's grasp and plunged on its own accord towards the heart of his opponent.

'No!' Elric tried to catch hold of his blade but could not. Stormbringer plunged into Nikorn's great heart and wailed in demoniac triumph. 'No!' Elric got hold of the hilt and tried to pull it from Nikorn. The merchant shrieked in hell-brought agony. He should have been dead.

He still half-lived.

'It's taking me – the thrice-damned thing is taking me!' Nikorn gurgled horribly, clutching at the black steel with hands turned to claws. 'Stop it, Elric – I beg you, stop it! *Please*!'

Elric tried again to tug the blade from Nikorn's heart. He could not. It was rooted in flesh, sinew and vitals. It moaned greedily, drinking into it all that was the being of Nikorn of Ilmar. It sucked the life-force from the dying man and all the while its voice was soft and disgustingly sensuous. Still Elric struggled to pull the sword free. It was impossible. 'Damn you!' he moaned. 'This man was almost my friend – I gave him my word not to kill him.' But Stormbringer, though sentient, could not hear its master.

Nikorn shrieked once more, the shriek dying to a low, lost whimper. And then his body died.

It died – and the soul-stuff of Nikorn joined the souls of the countless others, friends, kin and enemies who had gone to feed that which fed Elric of Melniboné.

Elric sobbed.

'Why is this curse upon me? Why?'

He collapsed to the ground in the dirt and the blood.

Minutes later, Moonglum came upon his friend lying face downward. He grasped Elric by his shoulders and turned him. He shuddered when he saw the albino's agony-racked face.

'What happened?'

Elric raised himself on one elbow and pointed to where Nikorn's body lay a few feet away. 'Another, Moonglum. Oh, curse this blade!'

Moonglum said uncomfortably: 'He would have killed

you no doubt. Do not think about it. Many a word's been broken through no-fault of he who gave it. Come, my friend, Yishana awaits us in the Tavern of the Purple Dove.'

Elric struggled upright and began to walk slowly towards the battered gates of the palace where horses awaited them.

As they rode for Bakshaan, not knowing what was troubling the people of that city, Elric tapped Stormbringer which hung, once more, at his side. His eyes were hard and moody, turned inwards on his own feelings.

'Be wary of this devil-blade, Moonglum. It kills the foe – but savours the blood of friends and kin-folk most.'

Moonglum shook his head quickly, as if to clear it, and looked away. He said nothing.

Elric made as if to speak again but then changed his mind. He needed to talk, then. He needed to – but there was nothing to say at all.

Pilarmo scowled. He stared, hurt-faced, as his slaves struggled with his chests of treasure, lugging them out to pile them in the street beside his great house. In other parts of the city, Pilarmo's three colleagues were also in various stages of heart-break. Their treasure, too, was being dealt with in a like manner. The burghers of Bakshaan had decided who was to pay any possible ransom.

And then a ragged citizen was shambling down the street, pointing behind him and shouting.

'The albino and his companion – at the North gate!'

The burghers who stood near to Pilarmo exchanged glances. Faratt swallowed.

He said: 'Elric comes to bargain. Quick. Open the treasure chests and tell the city guard to admit him.' One of the citizens scurried off.

Within a few minutes, while Faratt and the rest worked frantically to expose Pilarmo's treasure to the gaze of the approaching albino, Elric was galloping up the street,

Moonglum beside him. Both men were expressionless. They knew enough not to show their puzzlement.

'What's this?' Elric said, casting a look at Pilarmo.

Faratt cringed. 'Treasure,' he whined. 'Yours, Lord Elric – for you and your men. There's much more. There is no need to use sorcery. No need for your men to attack us. The treasure here is fabulous – its value is enormous. Will you take it and leave the city in peace?'

Moonglum almost smiled, but he controlled his features.

Elric said coolly: 'It will do. I accept it. Make sure this and the rest is delivered to my men at Nikorn's castle or we'll be roasting you and your friends over open fires by the morrow.'

Faratt coughed suddenly, trembling. 'As you say, Lord Elric. It shall be delivered.'

The two men wheeled their horses in the direction of the Tavern of the Purple Dove. When they were out of earshot Moonglum said: 'From what I gathered, back there, it's Master Pilarmo and his friends who are paying that unasked for toll.'

Elric was incapable of any real humour, but he half-chuckled. 'Aye. I'd planned to rob them from the start – and now their own fellows have done it for us. On our way back, we shall take our pick of the spoils.'

He rode on and reached the tavern. Yishana was waiting there, nervously, dressed for travelling.

When she saw Elric's face she sighed with satisfaction and smiled silkily. 'So Theleb K'aarna is dead,' she said. 'Now we can resume our interrupted relationship, Elric.'

The albino nodded. 'That was my part of the bargain – you kept yours when you helped Moonglum to get my sword back for me.' He showed no emotion.

She embraced him, but he drew back. 'Later,' he murmured. 'But that is one promise I shall not break, Yishana.'

He helped the puzzled woman mount her waiting horse.

They rode back towards Pilarmo's house.

She asked: 'And what of Nikorn – is he safe? I liked that man.'

'He died,' Elric's voice was strained.

'How?' she asked.

'Because, like all merchants,' Elric answered, 'he bargained too hard.'

There was an unnatural silence among the three as they made their horses speed faster towards the Gates of Bakshaan, and Elric did not stop when the others did, to take their pick of Pilarmo's riches. He rode on, unseeing, and the others had to spur their steeds in order to catch up with him, two miles beyond the city.

Over Bakshaan, no breeze stirred in the gardens of the rich. No winds came to blow cool on the sweating faces of the poor. Only the sun blazed in the heavens, round and red, and a shadow, shaped like a dragon, moved across it once, and then was gone.

BOOK TWO

Kings in Darkness

Three Kings in Darkness lie,
Gutheran of Org, and I,
Under a bleak and sunless sky—
The third Beneath the Hill.

—Song of Veerkad
by James Cawthorn.

1

Elric, Lord of the lost and sundered Empire of Melniboné, rode like a fanged wolf from a trap – all slavering madness and mirth. He rode from Nadsokor, City of Beggars, and there was hate in his wake for he had been recognized as their old enemy before he could obtain the secret he had sought there. Now they hounded him and the grotesque little man who rode laughing at Elric's side; Moonglum the Outlander, from Elwher and the unmapped East.

The flames of brands devoured the velvet of the night as the yelling, ragged throng pushed their bony nags in pursuit of the pair.

Starvelings and tattered jackals that they were, there was strength in their gaudy numbers and long knives and bone bows glinted in the brandlight. They were too strong for a couple of men to fight, too few to represent serious danger in a hunt, so Elric and Moonglum had chosen to leave the city without dispute and now sped towards the full and rising moon which stabbed its sickly beams through the darkness to show them the disturbing waters of the Varkalk River and a chance of escape from the incensed mob.

They had half a mind to stand and face the mob, since the Varkalk was their only alternative. But they knew well what the beggars would do to them, whereas they were uncertain what would become of them once they had entered the river. The horses reached the sloping banks of the Varkalk and reared, with hooves lashing.

Cursing, the two men spurred the steeds and forced them down towards the water. Into the river the horses plunged, snorting and spluttering. Into the river which led a roaring course towards the hell-spawned Forest of Troos which lay within the borders of Org, country of necromancy and rotting, ancient evil.

Elric blew water away from his mouth and coughed. 'They'll not follow us to Troos, I think,' he shouted at his companion.

Moonglum said nothing. He only grinned, showing his white teeth and the unhidden fear in his eyes. The horses swam strongly with the current and behind them the ragged mob shrieked in frustrated blood-lust while some of their number laughed and jeered.

'Let the forest do our work for us!'

Elric laughed back at them, wildly, as the horses swam on down the dark, straight river, wide and deep, towards a sun-starved morning, cold and spiky with ice. Scattered, slim-peaked crags loomed on either side of the flat plain, through which the river ran swiftly. Green-tinted masses of jutting blacks and browns spread colour through the rocks and the grass was waving on the plain as if for some purpose. Through the dawnlight, the beggar crew chased along the banks, but eventually gave up their quarry to return, shuddering, to Nadsokor.

When they had gone, Elric and Moonglum made their mounts swim towards the banks and climb them, stumbling, to the top where rocks and grass had already given way to sparse forest land which rose starkly on all sides, staining the earth with sombre shades. The foliage waved jerkily, as if alive – sentient.

It was a forest of malignantly erupting blooms, blood-coloured and sickly-mottled. A forest of bending, sinuously smooth trunks, black and shiny; a forest of spiked leaves of murky purples and gleaming greens – certainly an unhealthy place if judged only by the odour of rotting vegetation which was almost unbearable, impinging as it did upon the fastidious nostrils of Elric and Moonglum.

Moonglum wrinkled his nose and jerked his head in the direction they had come. 'Back now?' he inquired. 'We can avoid Troos and cut swiftly across a corner of Org to be in·

Bakshaan in just over a day. What say you, Elric?'

Elric frowned. 'I don't doubt they'd welcome us in Bakshaan with the same warmth we received in Nadsokor. They'll not have forgotten the destruction we wrought there – and the wealth we acquired from their merchants. No, I have a fancy to explore the forest a little. I have heard tales of Org and its unnatural forest and should like to investigate the truth of them. My blade and sorcery will protect us, if necessary.'

Moonglum sighed. 'Elric – this once, let us not court the danger.'

Elric smiled icily. His scarlet eyes blazed out of his dead white skin with peculiar intensity. 'Danger? It can bring only death.'

'Death is not to my liking, just yet,' Moonglum said. 'The fleshpots of Bakshaan, or if you prefer – Jadmar – on the other hand . . .'

But Elric was already urging his horse onward, heading for the forest. Moonglum sighed and followed.

Soon dark blossoms hid most of the sky, which was dark enough, and they could see only a little way in all directions. The rest of the forest seemed vast and sprawling; they could sense this, though sight of most of it was lost in the depressing gloom.

Moonglum recognized the forest from descriptions he had heard from mad-eyed travellers who drank purposefully in the shadows of Nadsokor's taverns.

'This is the Forest of Troos, sure enough,' he said to Elric. 'It's told of how the Doomed Folk released tremendous forces upon the earth and caused terrible changes among men, beasts and vegetation. This forest is the last they created, and the last to perish.'

'A child will always hate its parents at certain times,' Elric said mysteriously.

'Children of whom to be extremely wary, I should think,' Moonglum retorted. 'Some say that when they were at the

63

peak of their power, they had no Gods to frighten them.'

'A daring people, indeed,' Elric replied, with a faint smile. 'They have my respect. Now fear and the Gods are back and that, at least, is comforting.'

Moonglum puzzled over this for a short time, and then, eventually, said nothing.

He was beginning to feel uneasy.

The place was full of malicious rustlings and whispers, though no living animal inhabited it, as far as they could tell. There was a discomforting absence of birds, rodents or insects and, though they normally had no love for such creatures, they would have appreciated their company in the disconcerting forest.

In a quavering voice, Moonglum began to sing a song in the hope that it would keep his spirits up and his thoughts off the lurking forest.

'A grin and a word is my trade;
From these, my profit is made.
Though my body's not tall and my courage is small,
My fame will take longer to fade.'

So singing, with his natural amiability returning, Moonglum rode after the man he regarded as a friend – a friend who possessed something akin to mastery over him, though neither admitted it.

Elric smiled at Moonglum's song. 'To sing of one's own lack of size and absence of courage is not an action designed to ward off one's enemies, Moonglum.'

'But this way I offer no provocation,' Moonglum replied glibly. 'If I sing of my shortcomings, I am safe. If I were to boast of my talents, then someone might consider this to be a challenge and decide to teach me a lesson.'

'True,' Elric assented gravely, 'and well-spoken.'

He began pointing at certain blossoms and leaves, remarking upon their alien tint and texture, referring to them in words which Moonglum could not understand, though he knew the words to be part of a sorcerer's vocabulary. The albino seemed to be untroubled by the fears which beset the Eastlander, but often, Moonglum knew, appearances with Elric could hide the opposite of what they indicated.

They stopped for a short break while Elric sifted through some of the samples he had torn from trees and plants. He carefully placed his prizes in his belt-pouch but would say nothing of why he did so to Moonglum.

'Come,' he said, 'Troos's mysteries await us.'

But then a new voice, a woman's, said softly from the gloom: 'Save the excursion for another day, strangers.'

Elric reined his horse, one hand at Stormbringer's hilt. The voice had had an unusual effect upon him. It had been low, deep and had, for a moment, sent the pulse in his throat throbbing. Incredibly, he sensed that he was suddenly standing on one of Fate's roads, but where the road would take him, he did not know. Quickly, he controlled his mind and then his body and looked towards the shadows from where the voice had come.

'You are very kind to offer us advice, madam,' he said sternly. 'Come, show yourself and give explanation . . .'

She rode then, very slowly, on a black-coated gelding that pranced with a power she could barely restrain. Moonglum drew an appreciative breath for although heavy-featured, she was incredibly beautiful. Her face and bearing was patrician, her eyes were grey-green, combining enigma and innocence. She was very young. For all her obvious womanhood and beauty, Moonglum aged her at seventeen or little more.

Elric frowned: 'Do you ride alone?'

'I do now,' she replied, trying to hide her obvious astonishment at the albino's colouring. 'I need aid – protection. Men who will escort me safely to Karlaak. There, they will be paid.'

'Karlaak, by the Weeping Waste? It lies the other side of Ilmiora, a hundred leagues away and a week's travelling at speed.' Elric did not wait for her to reply to this statement. 'We are not hirelings, madam.'

'Then you are bound by the vows of chivalry, sir, and cannot refuse my request.'

Elric laughed shortly. 'Chivalry, madam? We come not from the upstart nations of the South with their strange codes and rules of behaviour. We are nobles of older stock whose actions are governed by our own desires. You would not ask what you do, if you knew our names.'

She wetted her full lips with her tongue and said almost timidly: 'You are . . .?'

'Elric of Melniboné, madam, called Elric Woman-slayer in the West, and this is Moonglum of Elwher; he has no conscience.'

She said: 'There are legends – the white-faced reaver, the hell-driven sorcerer with a blade that drinks the souls of men . . .'

'Aye, that's true. And however magnified they are with the retelling, they cannot hint, those tales, at the darker truths which lie in their origin. Now, madam, do you still seek our aid?' Elric's voice was gentle, without menace, as he saw that she was very much afraid, although she had managed to control the signs of fear and her lips were tight with determination.

'I have no choice. I am at your mercy. My father, the Senior Senator of Karlaak, is very rich. Karlaak is called the City of the Jade Towers, as you will know, and such rare jades and ambers we have. Many could be yours.'

'Be careful, madam, lest you anger me,' warned Elric, although Moonglum's bright eyes lighted with avarice. 'We are not nags to be hired or goods to be bought. Besides which,' he smiled disdainfully, 'I am from crumbling Imrryr, the Dreaming City, from the Isle of the Dragon, hub of Ancient Melniboné, and I know what beauty really is. Your baubles cannot tempt one who has looked upon the milky Heart of Arioch, upon the blinding iridescence that throbs from the Ruby Throne, of the languorous and unnameable colours in the Actorios stone of the Ring of Kings. These are more than jewels, madam – they contain the life-stuff of the universe.'

'I apologize, Lord Elric, and to you, Sir Moonglum.'

Elric laughed, almost with affection. 'We are grim clowns, lady, but the Gods of Luck aided our escape from Nadsokor and we owe them a debt. We'll escort you to Karlaak, City of the Jade Towers, and explore the Forest of Troos another time.'

Her thanks was tempered with a wary look in her eyes.

'And now we have made introductions,' said Elric, 'perhaps you would be good enough to give your name and tell us your story.'

'I am Zarozinia from Karlaak, a daughter of the Voashoon, the most powerful clan in South Eastern Ilmiora. We have kinsmen in the trading cities on the coasts of Pikarayd and I went with two cousins and my uncle to visit them.'

'A perilous journey, Lady Zarozinia.'

'Aye, and there are not only natural dangers, sir. Two weeks ago we made our goodbyes and began the journey home. Safely we crossed the Straits of Vilmir and there employed men-at-arms, forming a strong caravan to journey through Vilmir and so to Ilmiora. We skirted Nadsokor since we had heard that the City of Beggars is inhospitable to honest travellers . . .'

Here, Elric smiled: 'And sometimes to dishonest travellers, as we can appreciate.'

Again the expression on her face showed that she had some difficulty in equating his obvious good humour with his evil reputation. 'Having skirted Nadsokor,' she continued, 'we came this way and reached the borders of Org

67

wherein, of course, Troos lies. Very warily we travelled, knowing dark Org's reputation, along the fringes of the forest. And then we were ambushed and our hired men-at-arms deserted us.'

'Ambushed, eh?' broke in Moonglum. 'By whom, madam, did you know?'

'By their unsavoury looks and squat shapes they seemed natives. They fell upon the caravan and my uncle and cousins fought bravely but were slain. One of my cousins slapped the rump of my gelding and sent it galloping so that I could not control it. I heard – terrible screams – mad, giggling shouts – and when I at last brought my horse to a halt, I was lost. Later I heard you approach and waited in fear for you to pass, thinking you also were of Org, but when I heard your accents and some of your speech, I thought that you might help me.'

'And help you we shall, madam,' said Moonglum bowing gallantly from the saddle. 'And I am indebted to you for convincing Lord Elric here of your need. But for you, we should be deep in this awful forest by now and experiencing strange terrors no doubt. I offer my sorrow for your dead kinfolk and assure you that you will be protected from now onwards by more than swords and brave hearts, for sorcery can be called up if needs be.'

'Let's hope there'll be no need,' frowned Elric. 'You talk blithely of sorcery, friend Moonglum – you who hate the art.'

Moonglum grinned.

'I was consoling the young lady, Elric. And I've had occasion to be grateful for your horrid powers, I'll admit. Now I suggest that we make camp for the night and so refreshed be on our way at dawn.'

'I'll agree to that,' said Elric, glancing almost with embarrassment at the girl. Again he felt the pulse in his throat and this time he had more difficulty in controlling it.

The girl also seemed fascinated by the albino. There was

an attraction between them which might be strong enough to throw both their destinies along wildly different paths than any they had guessed.

Night came again quickly, for the days were short in those parts. While Moonglum tended the fire, nervously peering around him, Zarozinia, her richly embroidered cloth-of-gold gown shimmering in the firelight, walked gracefully to where Elric sat sorting the herbs he had collected. She glanced at him cautiously and then seeing that he was absorbed, stared at him with open curiosity.

He looked up and smiled faintly, his eyes for once unprotected, his strange face frank and pleasant. 'Some of these are healing herbs,' he said, 'and others are used in summoning spirits. Yet others give unnatural strength to the imbiber and some turn men mad. They will be useful to me.'

She sat down beside him, her thick-fingered hands pushing her black hair back. Her small breasts lifted and fell rapidly.

'Are you really the terrible evil-bringer of the legends, Lord Elric? I find it hard to credit.'

'I have brought evil to many places,' he said, 'but usually there has already been evil to match mine. I seek no excuses, for I know what I am and I know what I have done. I have slain malignant sorcerers and destroyed oppressors, but I have also been responsible for slaying fine men, and a woman, my cousin, whom I loved, I killed – or my sword did.'

'And you are master of your sword?'

'I often wonder. Without it, I am helpless.' He put his hand around Stormbringer's hilt. 'I should be grateful to it.' Once again his red eyes seemed to become deeper, protecting some bitter emotion rooted at the core of his soul.

'I'm sorry if I revived unpleasant recollection . . .'

69

'Do not feel sorry, Lady Zarozinia. The pain is within me – you did not put it there. In fact I'd say you relieve it greatly by your presence.'

Half-startled, she glanced at him and smiled. 'I am no wanton, sir,' she said, 'but . . .'

He got up quickly.

'Moonglum, is the fire going well?'

'Aye, Elric. She'll stay in for the night.' Moonglum cocked his head on one side. It was unlike Elric to make such empty queries, but Elric said nothing further so the Eastlander shrugged, turned away to check his gear.

Since he could think of little else to say, Elric turned and said quietly, urgently: 'I'm a killer and a thief, not fit to . . .'

'Lord Elric, I am . . .'

'You are infatuated by a legend, that is all.'

'No! If you feel what I feel, then you'll know it's more.'

'You are young.'

'Old enough.'

'Beware. I must fulfil my destiny.'

'Your destiny?'

'It is no destiny at all, but an awful thing called doom. And I have no pity except when I see something in my own soul. Then I have pity – and I pity. But I hate to look and this is part of the doom which drives me. Not Fate, nor the Stars, nor Men, nor Demons, nor Gods. Look at me, Zarozinia – it is Elric, poor white chosen plaything of the Gods of Time – Elric of Melniboné who causes his own gradual and terrible destruction.'

'It is suicide!'

'Aye. I drive myself to slow death. And those who go with me suffer also.'

'You speak falsely, Lord Elric – from guilt-madness.'

'Because I am guilty, lady.'

'And does Sir Moonglum go to doom with you?'

'He is unlike others – he is indestructible in his own self-assurance.'

70

'I am confident, also, Lord Elric.'

'But your confidence is that of youth, it is different.'

'Need I lose it with my youth?'

'You have strength. You are as strong as we are. I'll grant you that.'

She opened her arms, rising. 'Then be reconciled, Elric of Melniboné.'

And he was. He seized her, kissing her with a deeper need than that of passion. For the first time Cymoril of Imrryr was forgotten as they lay down, together on the soft turf, oblivious of Moonglum who polished away at his curved sword with wry jealousy.

They all slept and the fire waned.

Elric, in his joy, had forgotten, or not heeded, that he had a watch to take and Moonglum, who had no source of strength but himself, stayed awake for as long as he could but sleep overcame him.

In the shadows of the awful trees, figures moved with shambling caution.

The misshapen men of Org began to creep inwards towards the sleepers.

Then Elric opened his eyes, aroused by instinct, stared at Zarozinia's peaceful face beside him, moved his eyes without turning his head and saw the danger. He rolled over, grasped Stormbringer and tugged the runeblade from its sheath. The sword hummed, as if in anger at being awakened.

'Moonglum! Danger!' Elric bellowed in fear, for he had more to protect than his own life. The little man's head jerked up. His curved sabre was already across his knees and he jumped to his feet, ran towards Elric as the men of Org closed in.

'I apologize,' he said.

'My fault, I . . .'

And then the men of Org were at them. Elric and

71

Moonglum stood over the girl as she came awake, saw the situation and did not scream. Instead she looked around for a weapon but found none. She remained still, where she was, the only thing to do.

Smelling like offal, the gibbering creatures, some dozen of them, slashed at Elric and Moonglum with heavy blades like cleavers, long and dangerous.

Stormbringer whined and smote through a cleaver, cut into a neck and beheaded the owner. Blood gurgled from the corpse as it slumped back across the fire. Moonglum ducked beneath a howling cleaver, lost his balance, fell, slashed at his opponent's legs and ham-strung him so that he collapsed shrieking. Moonglum stayed on the ground and lunged upwards, taking another in the heart. Then he sprang to his feet and stood shoulder to shoulder with Elric while Zarozinia got up behind them.

'The horses,' grunted Elric. 'If it's safe, try to get them.'

There were still seven natives standing and Moonglum groaned as a cleaver sliced flesh from his left arm, retaliated, pierced the man's throat, turned slightly and sheared off another's face. They pressed forward, taking the attack to the incensed foe. His left hand covered with his own blood, Moonglum painfully pulled his long poignard from its sheath and held it with his thumb along the handle, blocked an opponent's swing, closed in and killed him with a ripping upward thrust of the dagger, the action of which caused his wound to pound with agony.

Elric held his great runesword in both hands and swung it in a semi-circle, hacking down the howling misshapen things. Zarozinia darted towards the horses, leaped on to her own and led the other two towards the fighting men. Elric smote at another and got into his saddle, thanking his own forethought to leave the equipment on the horses in case of danger. Moonglum quickly joined him and they thundered out of the clearing.

'The saddle-bags,' Moonglum called in greater agony

than that created by his wound. 'We've left the saddle-bags!'

'What of it? Don't press your luck, my friend.'

'But all our treasure's in them!'

Elric laughed, partly in relief, partly from real humour. 'We'll retrieve them, friend, never fear.'

'I know you, Elric. You've no value for the realities.'

But even Moonglum was laughing as they left the enraged men of Org behind them and slowed to a canter.

Elric reached and hugged Zarozinia. 'You have the courage of your noble clan in your veins,' he said.

'Thank you,' she replied, pleased with the compliment, 'but we cannot match such swordmanship as that displayed by you and Moonglum. It was fantastic.'

'Thank the blade,' he said shortly.

'No. I will thank you. I think you place too much reliance upon that hell weapon, however powerful it is.'

'I need it.'

'For what?'

'For my own strength and, now, to give strength to you.'

'I'm no vampire,' she smiled, 'and need no such fearful strength as that supplies.'

'Then be assured that I do,' he told her gravely. 'You would not love me if the blade did not give me what I need. I am like a spineless sea-thing without it.'

'I do not believe that, but will not dispute with you now.'

They rode for a while without speaking.

Later, they stopped, dismounted, and Zarozinia put herbs that Elric had given her upon Moonglum's wounded arm and began to bind it.

Elric was thinking deeply. The forest rustled with macabre, sensuous sounds. 'We're in the heart of Troos,' he said, 'and our intention to skirt the forest has been forestalled. I have it in mind to call on the King of Org and so round off our visit.'

Moonglum laughed. 'Shall we send our swords along

first? And bind our own hands?' His pain was already eased by the herbs which were having quick effect.

'I mean it. We owe, all of us, much to the men of Org. They slew Zarozinia's uncle and cousins, they wounded you and they now have our treasure. We have many reasons for asking the King for recompense. Also, they seem stupid and should be easy to trick.'

'Aye. The King will pay us back for our lack of common-sense by tearing our limbs off.'

'I'm in earnest. I think we should go.'

'I'll agree that I'd like our wealth returned to us. But we cannot risk the lady's safety, Elric.'

'I am to be Elric's wife, Moonglum. Therefore if he visits the King of Org, I shall come too.'

Moonglum lifted an eyebrow. 'A quick courtship.'

'She speaks the truth, however. We shall all go to Org – and sorcery will protect us from the King's uncalled-for wrath.'

'And still you wish for death and vengeance, Elric,' shrugged Moonglum mounting. 'Well, it's all the same to me since your roads, whatever else, are profitable ones. You may be the Lord of Bad Luck by your own reckoning, but you bring good luck to me, I'll say that.'

'No more courting death,' smiled Elric, 'but we'll have some revenge, I hope.'

'Dawn will be with us soon,' Moonglum said. 'The Orgian citadel lies six hours' ride from here by my working, south-south-east by the Ancient Star, if the map I memorized in Nadsokor was correct.'

'You have an instinct for direction that never fails, Moonglum. Every caravan should have such a man as you.'

'We base an entire philosophy on the stars in Elwher,' Moonglum replied. 'We regard them as the master plan for everything that happens on Earth. As they revolve around the planet they see all things, past, present and future. They are our Gods.'

'Predictable Gods, at least,' said Elric and they rode off towards Org with light hearts considering the enormity of their risk.

2

Little was known of the tiny kingdom of Org save that the Forest of Troos lay within its boundaries and to that, other nations felt, it was welcome. The people were unpleasant to look upon, for the most part, and their bodies were stunted and strangely altered. Legend had it that they were the descendants of the Doomed Folk. Their rulers, it was said, were shaped like normal men in so far as their outward bodily appearance went, but their minds were warped more horribly than the limbs of their subjects.

The inhabitants were few and were generally scattered, ruled by their king from his citadel which was also called Org.

It was for this citadel that Elric and his companions rode and, as they did so, Elric explained how he planned to protect them all from the natives of Org.

In the forest he had found a particular leaf which, when used with certain invocations (which were harmless in that the invoker was in little danger of being harmed by the spirits he marshalled) would invest that person, and anyone else to whom he gave the drug distilled from the leaf, with temporary invulnerability.

The spell somehow reknitted the skin and flesh structure so that it could withstand any edge and almost any blow. Elric explained, in a rare garrulous mood, how the drug and spell combined to achieve the effect, but his archaicisms and esoteric words meant little to the other two.

They stopped an hour's ride from where Moonglum expected to find the citadel so that Elric could prepare the drug and invoke the spell.

He worked swiftly over a small fire, using an alchemist's

pestle and mortar, mixing the shredded leaf with a little water. As the brew bubbled on the fire, he drew peculiar runes on the ground, some of which were twisted into such alien forms that they seemed to disappear into a different dimension and reappear beyond it.

> *'Bone and blood and flesh and sinew,*
> *Spell and spirit bind anew;*
> *Potent potion work the life charm,*
> *Keep its takers safe from harm.'*

So Elric chanted as a small pink cloud formed in the air over the fire, wavered, reformed into a spiral shape which curled downwards into the bowl. The brew spluttered and then was still. The albino sorcerer said: 'An old boyhood spell, so simple that I'd near forgotten it. The leaf for the potion grows only in Troos and therefore it is rarely possible to perform.'

The brew, which had been liquid, had now solidified and Elric broke it into small pellets. 'Too much,' he warned, 'taken at one time is poison, and yet the effect can last for several hours. Not always, though, but we must accept that small risk.' He handed both of them a pellet which they received dubiously. 'Swallow them just before we reach the citadel,' he told them, 'or in the event of the men of Org finding us first.'

Then they mounted and rode on again.

Some miles to the south-east of Troos, a blind man sang a grim song in his sleep and so woke himself . . .

They reached the brooding citadel of Org at dusk. Guttural voices shouted at them from the battlements of the square-cut ancient dwelling place of the Kings of Org. The thick rock oozed moisture and was corroded by lichen and sickly, mottle moss. The only entrance large enough for a mounted man to pass through was reached by a path almost a foot deep in evil-smelling black mud.

77

'What's your business at the Royal Court of Gutheran the Mighty?'

They could not see who asked the question.

'We seek hospitality and an audience with your liege,' called Moonglum cheerfully, successfully hiding his nervousness. 'We bring important news to Org.'

A twisted face peered down from the battlements. 'Enter strangers and be welcome,' it said unwelcomingly.

The heavy wooden drawgate shifted upwards to allow them entrance and the horses pushed their way slowly through the mud and so into the courtyard of the citadel.

Overhead, the grey sky was a racing field of black tattered clouds which streamed towards the horizon as if to escape the horrid boundaries of Org and the disgusting Forest of Troos.

The courtyard was covered, though not so deeply, with the same foul mud as had impaired their progress to the citadel. It was full of heavy, unmoving shadow. On Elric's right, a flight of steps went up to an arched entrance which was hung, partially, with the same unhealthy lichen he had seen on the outer walls and, also, in the Forest of Troos.

Through this archway, brushing at the lichen with a pale, beringed hand, a tall man came and stood on the top step, regarding the visitors through heavy-lidded eyes. He was, in contrast to the others, handsome, with a massive, leonine head and long hair as white as Elric's; although the hair on the head of this great, solid man was somewhat dirty, tangled, unbrushed. He was dressed in a heavy jerkin of quilted, embossed leather, a yellow kilt which reached to his ankles and he carried a wide-bladed dagger, naked in his belt. He was older than Elric, aged between forty and fifty and his powerful if somewhat decadent face was seamed and pock-marked.

He stared at them in silence and did not welcome them; instead he signed to one of the battlement guards who caused the drawgate to be lowered. It came down with a

78

crash, blocking off their way of escape.

'Kill the men and keep the woman,' said the massive man in a low monotone. Elric had heard dead men speak in that manner.

As planned, Elric and Moonglum stood either side of Zarozinia and remained where they were, arms folded.

Puzzled, shambling creatures came warily at them, their loose trousers dragging in the mud, their hands hidden by the long shapeless sleeves of their filthy garments. They swung their cleavers. Elric felt a faint shock as the blade thudded on to his arm, but that was all. Moonglum's experience was similar.

The men fell back, amazement and confusion on their bestial faces.

The tall man's eyes widened. He put one ring-covered hand to his thick lips, chewing at a nail.

'Our swords have no effect upon them, King! They do not cut and they do not bleed. What are these folk?'

Elric laughed theatrically. 'We are not common folk, little human, be assured. We are the messengers of the Gods and come to your King with a message from our great masters. Do not worry, we shall not harm you since we are in no danger of being harmed. Stand aside and make us welcome.'

Elric could see that King Gutheran was puzzled and not absolutely taken in by his words. Elric cursed to himself. He had measured their intelligence by those he had seen. This king, mad or not, was much more intelligent, was going to be harder to deceive. He led the way up the steps towards glowering Gutheran.

'Greetings, King Gutheran. The Gods have, at last, returned to Org and wish you to know this.'

'Org has had no Gods to worship for an eternity,' said Gutheran hollowly, turning back into the citadel. 'Why should we accept them now?'

'You are impertinent, King.'

79

'And you are audacious. How do I know you come from the Gods?' He walked ahead of them, leading them through the low-roofed halls.

'You saw that the swords of your subjects had no effect upon us.'

'True. I'll take that incident as proof for the moment. I suppose there must be a banquet in your – honour – I shall order it. Be welcome, messengers.' His words were ungracious but it was virtually impossible to detect anything from Gutheran's tone, since the man's voice stayed at the same pitch.

Elric pushed his heavy riding cloak back from his shoulders and said lightly: 'We shall mention your kindness to our masters.'

The Court was a place of gloomy halls and false laughter and although Elric put many questions to Gutheran, the king would not answer them, or did so by means of ambiguous phrases which meant nothing. They were not given chambers wherein they could refresh themselves but instead stood about for several hours in the main hall of the citadel and Gutheran, while he was with them and not giving orders for the banquet, sat slumped on his throne and chewed at his nails, ignoring them.

'Pleasant hospitality,' whispered Moonglum.

'Elric – how long will the effects of the drug last?' Zarozinia had remained close to him. He put his arm around her shoulders. 'I do not know. Not much longer. But it has served its purpose. I doubt if they will try to attack us a second time. However, beware of other attempts, subtler ones, upon our lives.'

The main hall, which had a higher roof than the others and was completely surrounded by a gallery which ran around it well above the floor, fairly close to the room, was chilly and unwarmed. No fires burned in the several hearths, which were open and let into the floor, and the walls dripped moisture and were undecorated; damp, solid stone, timeworn and gaunt. There were not even rushes upon the floor which was strewn with old bones and pieces of decaying food.

'Hardly house-proud, are they?' commented Moonglum looking around him with distaste and glancing at brooding Gutheran who was seemingly oblivious of their presence.

A servitor shambled into the hall and whispered a few words to the king. He nodded and arose, leaving the Great Hall.

Soon men came in, carrying benches and tables and began to place them about the hall.

The banquet was, at last, due to commence. And the air had menace in it.

The three visitors sat together on the right of the King who had donned a richly jewelled chain of kingship, whilst his son and several pale-faced female members of the Royal line sat on the left, unspeaking even among themselves.

Prince Hurd, a sullen-faced youth who seemed to bear a resentment against his father, picked at the unappetizing food which was served them all.

He drank heavily of the wine which had little flavour but was strong, fiery stuff and this seemed to warm the company a little.

'And what do the Gods want of us poor folk of Org?' Hurd said, staring hard at Zarozinia with more than friendly interest.

Elric answered: 'They ask nothing of you but your recognition. In return they will, on occasions, help you.'

'That is all?' Hurd laughed. 'That is more than those from the Hill can offer, eh, father?'

Gutheran turned his great head slowly to regard his son.

'Yes,' he murmured, and the word seemed to carry warning.

Moonglum said: 'The Hill – what is that?'

He got no reply. Instead a high-pitched laugh came from

81

the entrance to the Great Hall. A thin, gaunt man stood there staring ahead with a fixed gaze. His features, though emaciated, strongly resembled Gutheran's. He carried a stringed instrument and plucked at the gut so that it wailed and moaned with melancholy insistence.

Hurd said savagely: 'Look, father, 'tis blind Veerkad, the minstrel, your brother. Shall he sing for us?'

'Sing?'

'Shall he sing his songs, father'

Gutheran's mouth trembled and twisted and he said after a moment: 'He may entertain our guests with an heroic ballad if he wishes, but . . .'

'But certain other songs he shall not sing . . .' Hurd grinned maliciously. He seemed to be tormenting his father deliberately in some way which Elric could not guess. Hurd shouted at the blind man: 'Come Uncle Veerkad – sing!'

'There are strangers present,' said Veerkad hollowly above the wail of his own music. 'Strangers in Org.'

Hurd giggled and drank more wine. Gutheran scowled and continued to tremble, gnawing at his nails.

Elric called: 'We'd appreciate a song, minstrel.'

'Then you'll have the song of the Three Kings in Darkness, strangers, and hear the ghastly story of the Kings of Org.'

'No!' shouted Gutheran, leaping from his place, but Veerkad was already singing:

> 'Three Kings in darkness lie,
> Gutheran of Org, and I,
> Under a bleak and sunless sky –
> The third beneath the Hill.
> When shall the third arise
> Only when another dies . . .'

'Stop!' Gutheran got up in an obviously insane rage and stumbled across the table, trembling in terror, his face blanched, striking at the blind man, his brother. Two blows and the minstrel fell, slumping to the floor and not moving. 'Take him out! Do not let him enter again.' The king shrieked and foam flecked his lips.

Hurd, sober for a moment, jumped across the table, scattering dishes and cups and took his father's arm.

'Be calm, father. I have a new plan for our entertainment.'

'You! You seek my throne. 'Twas you who goaded Veerkad to sing his dreadful song. You know I cannot listen without . . .' He stared at the door. 'One day the legend shall be realized and the Hill-King shall come. Then shall I, you and Org perish.'

'Father,' Hurd was smiling horribly, 'let the female visitor dance for us a dance of the Gods.'

'What?'

'Let the woman dance for us, father.'

Elric heard him. By now the drug must have worn off. He could not afford to show his hand by offering his companions further doses. He got to his feet.

'What sacrilege do you speak, Prince.'

'We have given you entertainment. It is the custom in Org for our visitors to give us entertainment also.'

The hall was filled with menace. Elric regretted his plan to trick the men of Org. But there was nothing he could do. He had intended to exact tribute from them in the name of the Gods, but obviously these mad men feared more immediate and tangible dangers than any the Gods might represent.

He had made a mistake, put the lives of his friends in danger as well as his own. What should he do? Zarozinia murmured: 'I have learned dances in Ilmiora where all ladies are taught the art. Let me dance for them. It might placate them and bedazzle them to make our work easier.'

'Arioch knows our work is hard enough now. I was a fool to have conceived this plan. Very well, Zarozinia, dance for them, but with caution.' He shouted at Hurd:

83

'Our companion will dance for you, to show you the beauty that the Gods create. Then you must pay the tribute, for our masters grow impatient.'

'The tribute?' Gutheran looked up. 'You mentioned nothing of tribute.'

'Your recognition of the Gods must take the form of precious stones and metals, King Gutheran. I thought you to understand that.'

'You seem more like common thieves than uncommon messengers, my friends. We are poor in Org and have nothing to give away to charlatans.'

'Beware of your words, King!' Elric's clear voice echoed warningly through the hall.

'We'll see the dance and then judge the truth of what you've told us.'

Elric seated himself, grasped Zarozinia's hand beneath the table as she arose, giving her comfort.

She walked gracefully and confidently into the centre of the hall and there began to dance. Elric, who loved her, was amazed at her splendid grace and artistry. She danced the old, beautiful dances of Ilmiora, entrancing even the thick-skulled men of Org and, as she danced, a great golden Guest Cup was brought in.

Hurd leaned across his father and said to Elric: 'The Guest Cup, Lord. It is our custom that our guests drink from it in friendship.'

Elric nodded, annoyed at being disturbed in his watching of the wonderful dance, his eyes fixed on Zarozinia as she postured and glided. There was silence in the hall.

Hurd handed him the cup and absently he put it to his lips, seeing this Zarozinia danced on to the table and began to weave along it to where Elric sat. As he took the first sip, Zarozinia cried out and, with her foot, knocked the cup from his hand. The wine splashed on to Gutheran and Hurd who half rose, startled. 'It was drugged, Elric. They drugged it!'

Hurd lashed at her with his hand, striking her across the face. She fell from the table and lay moaning slightly on the filthy floor. 'Bitch! Would the messengers of the Gods be harmed by a little drugged wine?'

Enraged, Elric pushed aside Gutheran and struck savagely at Hurd so that the young man's mouth gushed blood. But the drug was already having effect. Gutheran shouted something and Moonglum drew his sabre, glancing upwards. Elric was swaying, his senses were jumbled and the scene had an unreal quality. He saw servants grasp Zarozinia but could not see how Moonglum was faring. He felt sick and dizzy, could hardly control his limbs.

Summoning up his last remaining strength, Elric clubbed Hurd down with one tremendous blow. Then he collapsed into unconsciousness.

3

There was the cold clutch of chains about his wrists and a thin drizzle was falling directly on to his face which stung where Hurd's nails had ripped it.

He looked about him. He was chained between two stone menhirs upon an obvious burial barrow of gigantic size. It was night and a pale moon hovered in the heavens above him. He looked down at the group of men below. Hurd and Gutheran were among them. They grinned at him mockingly.

'Farewell, messenger. You will serve us a good purpose and placate the Ones from the Hill!' Hurd called as he and the others scurried back towards the citadel which lay, silhouetted, a short distance away.

Where was he? What had happened to Zarozinia – and Moonglum? Why had he been chained thus upon – realization and remembrance came – *the Hill!*

He shuddered, helpless in the strong chains which held him. Desperately he began to tug at them, but they would not yield. He searched his brain for a plan, but he was confused by torment and worry for his friends' safety. He heard a dreadful scuttling sound from below and saw a ghastly white shape dart into the gloom. Wildly he struggled in the rattling iron which held him.

In the Great Hall of the citadel, a riotous celebration was now reaching the state of an ecstatic orgy. Gutheran and Hurd were totally drunk, laughing insanely at their victory.

Outside the Hall, Veerkad listened and hated. Particularly he hated his brother, the man who had deposed and blinded him to prevent his study of sorcery by means of which he had planned to raise the King from Beneath the Hill.

'The time has come, at last,' he whispered to himself and stopped a passing servant.

'Tell me – where is the girl kept?'

'In Gutheran's chamber, master.'

Veerkad released the man and began to grope his way through the gloomy corridors up twisting steps, until he reached the room he sought. Here he produced a key, one of many he'd had made without Gutheran's knowing, and unlocked the door.

Zarozinia saw the blind man enter and could do nothing. She was gagged and bound with her own dress and still dazed from the blow Hurd had given her. They had told her of Elric's fate, but Moonglum had so far escaped them, guards hunted him now in the stinking corridors of Org.

'I've come to take you to your companion, lady,' smiled blind Veerkad, grasping her roughly with strength that his insanity had given him, picked her up and fumbled his way towards the door. He knew the passages of Org perfectly, for he had been born and grown up among them.

But two men were in the corridor outside Gutheran's chambers. One of them was Hurd, Prince of Org, who resented his father's appropriation of the girl and desired her for himself. He saw Veerkad bearing the girl away and stood silent while his uncle passed.

The other man was Moonglum, who observed what was happening from the shadows where he had hidden from the searching guards. As Hurd followed Veerkad, on cautious feet, Moonglum followed him.

Veerkad went out of the citadel by a small side door and carried his living burden towards the looming Burial Hill.

All about the foot of the monstrous barrow swarmed the leprous-white ghouls who sensed the presence of Elric, the folk of Org's sacrifice to them.

Now Elric understood.

These were the things that Org feared more than the Gods. These were the living-dead ancestors of those who now revelled in the Great Hall. Perhaps these were actually the Doomed Folk. Was that their doom? Never to rest? Never to die? Just to degenerate into mindless ghouls? Elric shuddered.

Now desperation brought back his memory. His voice was an agonized wail to the brooding sky and the pulsing earth.

'Arioch! Destroy the stones. Save your servant! Arioch – master – aid me!'

It was not enough. The ghouls gathered together and began to scuttle, gibbering up the barrow towards the helpless albino.

'Arioch! *These are the things that would forsake your memory! Aid me to destroy them!*'

The earth trembled and the sky became overcast, hiding the moon but not the white-faced, bloodless ghouls who were now almost upon him.

And then a ball of fire formed in the sky above him and the very sky seemed to shake and sway around it. Then, with a roaring crash two bolts of lightning slashed down, pulverizing the stones and releasing Elric.

He got to his feet, knowing that Arioch would demand his price, as the first ghouls reached him.

He did not retreat, but in his rage and desperation leapt among them, smashing and flailing with the lengths of chain. The ghouls fell back and fled, gibbering in fear and anger, down the hill and into the barrow.

Elric could now see that there was a gaping entrance to the barrow below him; black against the blackness. Breathing heavily, he found that his belt-pouch had been left him. From it he took a length of slim, gold wire and began frantically to pick at the locks of the manacles.

Veerkad chuckled to himself and Zarozinia hearing him was almost mad with terror. He kept drooling the words into her ear: 'When shall the third arise? Only when the other dies. When that other's blood flows red – we'll hear the footfalls of the dead. You and I, we shall resurrect him and such vengeance will he wreak upon my cursed brother. Your blood, my dear, it will be that which releases him.' He felt that the ghouls were gone and judged them placated by their feast. 'Your lover has been useful to me,' he laughed as he began to enter the barrow. The smell of death almost overpowered the girl as the blind madman bore her downwards into the heart of the Hill.

Hurd, sobered after his walk in the colder air, was horrified when he saw where Veerkad was going; the barrow, the Hill of the King, was the most feared spot in the land of Org. Hurd paused before the black entrance and turned to run. Then, suddenly, he saw the form of Elric, looming huge and bloody, descending the barrow slope, cutting off his escape.

With a wild yell he fled into the Hill passage.

Elric had not previously noticed the Prince, but the yell startled him and he tried to see who had given it but was too late. He began to run down the steep incline towards the entrance of the barrow. Another figure came scampering out of the darkness.

'Elric! Thank the stars and all the Gods of Earth! You live!'

'Thank Arioch, Moonglum. Where's Zarozinia?'

'In there – the mad minstrel took her with him and Hurd followed. They are all insane, these kings and princes, I see no sense to their actions.'

'I have an idea that the minstrel means Zarozinia no good. Quickly, we must follow.'

'By the stars, the stench of death! I have breathed nothing like it – not even at the great battle of the Eshmir Valley where the armies of Elwher met those of Kaleg Vogun, usurper prince of the Tanghensi, and half a million corpses strewed the valley from end to end.'

'If you've no stomach . . .'

'I wish I had none. It would not be so bad. Come . . .'

They rushed into the passage, led by the far away sounds of Veerkad's maniacal laughter and the somewhat nearer movements of a fear-maddened Hurd who was now trapped between two enemies and yet more afraid of a third.

Hurd blundered along in the blackness, sobbing to himself in his terror.

In the phosphorescent Central Tomb, surrounded by the mummified corpses of his ancestors, Veerkad chanted the resurrection ritual before the great coffin of the Hill-King – a giant thing, half as tall again as Veerkad who was tall enough. Veerkad was forgetful for his own safety and thinking only of vengeance upon his brother Gutheran. He held a long dagger over Zarozinia who lay huddled and terrified upon the ground near the coffin.

The spilling of Zarozinia's blood would be the culmination of the ritual and then—

Then Hell would, quite literally, be let loose. Or so Veerkad planned. He finished his chanting and raised the knife just as Hurd came screeching into the Central Tomb with his own sword drawn. Veerkad swung round, his blind face working in thwarted rage.

Savagely, without stopping for a moment, Hurd ran his sword into Veerkad's body, plunging the blade in up to the hilt so that its bloody point appeared sticking from his back. But the other, in his groaning death spasms, locked his hands about the Prince's throat. Locked them immovably.

Somehow, the two men retained a semblance of life and, struggling with each other in a macabre death-dance, swayed about the glowing chamber. The coffin of the Hill-King began to tremble and shake slightly, the movement hardly perceptible.

So Elric and Moonglum found Veerkad and Hurd. Seeing that both were near dead, Elric raced across the

Central Tomb to where Zarozinia lay, unconscious, mercifully, from her ordeal. Elric picked her up and made to return.

He glanced at the throbbing coffin.

'Quickly, Moonglum. That blind fool has invoked the dead, I can tell. Hurry, my friend, before the hosts of Hell are upon us.'

Moonglum gasped and followed Elric as he ran back towards the cleaner air of night.

'Where to now, Elric?'

'We'll have to risk going back to the citadel. Our horses are there and our goods. We need the horses to take us quickly away, for I fear there's going to be a terrible bloodletting soon if my instinct is right.'

'There should not be too much opposition, Elric. They were all drunk when I left. That was how I managed to evade them so easily. By now, if they continued drinking as heavily as when last I saw them, they'll be unable to move at all.'

'Then let's make haste.'

They left the Hill behind them and began to run towards the citadel.

4

Moonglum had spoken truth. Everyone was lying about the Great Hall in drunken sleep. Open fires had been lit in the hearths and they blazed, sending shadows skipping around the Hall. Elric said softly:

'Moonglum, go with Zarozinia to the stables and prepare our horses. I will settle our debt with Gutheran first.' He pointed. 'See, they have heaped their booty upon the table, gloating in their apparent victory.'

Stormbringer lay upon a pile of burst sacks and saddle-bags which contained the loot stolen from Zarozinia's uncle and cousins and from Elric and Moonglum.

Zarozinia, now conscious but confused, left with Moonglum to locate the stables and Elric picked his way towards the table, across the sprawled shapes of drunken men of Org, around the blazing fires and caught up, thankfully, his hell-forged runeblade.

Then he leaped over the table and was about to grasp Gutheran, who still had his fabulously gemmed chain of kingship around his neck, when the great doors of the Hall crashed open and a howling blast of icy air sent the torches dancing and leaping. Elric turned, Gutheran forgotten, and his eyes widened.

Framed in the doorway stood the King from Beneath the Hill.

The long-dead monarch had been raised by Veerkad whose own blood had completed the work of resurrection. He stood in rotting robes, his fleshless bones covered by tight, tattered skin. His heart did not beat, for he had none; he drew no breath, for his lungs had been eaten by the creatures which feasted on such things. But, horribly, he lived . . .

The King from the Hill. He had been the last great ruler of the Doomed Folk who had, in their fury, destroyed half the Earth and created the Forest of Troos. Behind the dead King crowded the ghastly hosts who had been buried with him in a legendary past.

The massacre began!

What secret vengeance was being reaped, Elric could only guess at – but whatever the reason, the danger was still very real.

Elric pulled out Stormbringer as the awakened horde vented their anger upon the living. The Hall became filled with the shrieking, horrified screams of the unfortunate Orgians. Elric remained, half-paralysed in his horror, beside the throne. Aroused, Gutheran woke up and saw the King from the Hill and his host. He screamed, almost thankfully:

'At last I can rest!'

And fell dying in a seizure, robbing Elric of his vengeance.

Veerkad's grim song echoed in Elric's memory. The Three Kings in Darkness – Gutheran, Veerkad and the King from Beneath the Hill. Now only the last lived – and he had been dead for millennia.

The King's cold, dead eyes roved the Hall and saw Gutheran sprawled upon his throne, the ancient chain of office still about his throat. Elric wrenched it off the body and backed away as the King from Beneath the Hill advanced. And then his back was against a pillar and there were feasting ghouls everywhere else.

The dead King came nearer and then, with a whistling moan which came from the depths of his decaying body, launched himself at Elric who found himself fighting desperately against the Hill-King's clawing, abnormal strength, cutting at flesh that neither bled nor suffered pain. Even the sorcerous runeblade could do nothing against this horror that had no soul to take and no blood to let.

Frantically, Elric slashed and hacked at the Hill-King but ragged nails raked his flesh and teeth snapped at his throat. And above everything came the almost overpowering stench of death as the ghouls, packing the Great Hall with their horrible shapes, feasted on the living and the dead.

Then Elric heard Moonglum's voice calling and saw him upon the gallery which ran around the Hall. He held a great oil jar.

'Lure him close to the central fire, Elric. There may be a way to vanquish him. Quickly man, or you're finished!'

In a frantic burst of energy, the Melnibonéan forced the giant king towards the flames. Around them, the ghouls fed off the remains of their victims, some of whom still lived, their screams calling hopelessly over the sound of carnage.

The Hill-King now stood, unfeeling, with his back to the leaping central fire. He still slashed at Elric. Moonglum hurled the jar.

It shattered upon the stone hearth, spraying the King with blazing oil. He staggered, and Elric struck with his full power, the man and the blade combining to push the Hill-King backwards. Down went the King into the flames and the flames began to devour him.

A dreadful, lost howling came from the burning giant as he perished.

Flames licked everywhere throughout the Great Hall and soon the place was like Hell itself, an inferno of licking fire through which the ghouls ran about, still feasting, unaware of their destruction. The way to the door was blocked.

Elric stared around him and saw no way of escape – save one.

Sheathing Stormbringer, he ran a few paces and leaped upwards, just grasping the rail of the gallery as flames engulfed the spot where he had been standing.

Moonglum reached down and helped him to clamber across the rail.

'I'm disappointed, Elric,' he grinned, 'you forgot to bring

the treasure.'

Elric showed him what he grasped in his left hand – the jewel-encrusted chain of kingship.

'This bauble is some reward for our hardships,' he smiled, holding up the glittering chain. 'I stole nothing, by Arioch! There are no kings left in Org to wear it! Come let's join Zarozinia and get our horses.'

They ran from the gallery as masonry began to crash downwards into the Great Hall.

They rode fast away from the halls of Org and looking back saw great fissures appear in the walls and heard the roar of destruction as the flames consumed everything that had been Org. They destroyed the seat of the monarchy, the remains of the Three Kings in Darkness, the present and the past. Nothing would be left of Org save an empty burial mound and two corpses, locked together, lying where their ancestors had lain for centuries in the Central Tomb. They destroyed the last link with the previous age and cleansed the Earth of an ancient evil. Only the dreadful Forest of Troos remained to mark the coming and the passing of the Doomed Folk.

And the Forest of Troos was a warning.

Weary and yet relieved, the three saw the outlines of Troos in the distance, behind the blazing funeral pyre.

And yet, in his happiness, Elric had a fresh problem on his mind now that danger was past.

'Why do you frown now, love?' asked Zarozinia.

'Because I think you spoke the truth. Remember you said I placed too much reliance on my runeblade here?'

'Yes – and I said I would not dispute with you.'

'Agreed. But I have a feeling that you were partially right. On the burial mound and in it I did not have Stormbringer with me – and yet I fought and won, because I feared for your safety.' His voice was quiet. 'Perhaps, in time, I can keep my strength by means of certain herbs I found in Troos and dispense with the blade for ever?'

95

Moonglum shouted with laughter hearing these words.

'Elric – I never thought I'd witness this. You daring to think of dispensing with that foul weapon of yours. I don't know if you ever shall, but the thought is comforting.'

'It is, my friend, it is.' He leaned in his saddle and grasped Zarozinia's shoulders, pulling her dangerously towards him as they galloped without slackening speed. And as they rode he kissed her, heedless of their pace.

'A new beginning!' he shouted above the wind. 'A new beginning, my love!'

And then they all rode laughing towards Karlaak by the Weeping Waste, to present themselves, to enrich themselves, and to attend the strangest wedding the Northern Lands had ever witnessed.

BOOK THREE

The Flamebringers

In which Moonglum returns from the Eastlands with
disturbing news . . .

1

Bloody-beaked hawks soared on the frigid wind. They soared high above a mounted horde inexorably moving across the Weeping Waste.

The horde had crossed two deserts and three mountain ranges to be there and hunger drove them onwards. They were spurred on by remembrances of stories heard from travellers who had come to their Eastern homeland, by the encouragements of their thin-lipped leader who swaggered in his saddle ahead of them, one arm wrapped around a ten-foot lance decorated with the gory trophies of his pillaging campaigns.

The riders moved slowly and wearily, unaware that they were nearing their goal.

Far behind the horde, a stocky rider left Elwher, the singing, boisterous capital of the Eastern world, and came soon to a valley.

The hard skeletons of trees had a blighted look and the horse kicked earth the colour of ashes as its rider drove it fiercely through the sick wasteland that had once been gentle Eshmir, the golden garden of the East.

A plague had smitten Eshmir and the locust had stripped her of her beauty. Both plague and locust went by the same name – Terarn Gashtek, Lord of the Mounted Hordes, sunken-faced carrier of destruction; Terarn Gashtek, insane blood-drawer, the shrieking flame bringer. And that was his other name – Flame Bringer.

The rider who witnessed the evil that Terarn Gashtek had brought to gentle Eshmir was named Moonglum. Moonglum was riding, now, for Karlaak by the Weeping Waste, the last outpost of the Western civilization of which those in the Eastlands knew little. In Karlaak, Moonglum knew he would find Elric of Melniboné who now dwelt permanently in his wife's graceful city. Moonglum was desperate to reach Karlaak quickly, to warn Elric and to solicit his help.

He was small and cocky, with a broad mouth and a shock of red hair, but now his mouth did not grin and his body was bent over the horse as he pushed it on towards Karlaak. For Eshmir, gentle Eshmir, had been Moonglum's home province and, with his ancestors, had formed him into what he was.

So, cursing, Moonglum rode for Karlaak.

But so did Terarn Gashtek. And already the Flame Bringer had reached the Weeping Waste. The horde moved slowly, for they had wagons with them which had at one time dropped far behind but now the supplies they carried were needed. As well as provisions, one of the wagons carried a bound prisoner who lay on his back cursing Terarn Gashtek and his slant-eyed battlemongers.

Drinij Bara was bound by more than strips of leather, that was why he cursed, for Drinij Bara was a sorcerer who could not normally be held in such a manner. If he had not succumbed to his weakness for wine and women just before the Flame Bringer had come down on the town in which he was staying, he would not have been trussed so, and Terarn Gashtek would not now have Drinij Bara's soul.

Drinij Bara's soul reposed in the body of a small, black cat – the cat which Terarn Gashtek had caught and carried with him always, for, as was the habit of Eastern sorcerers, Drinij Bara had hidden his soul in the body of the cat for protection. Because of this he was now slave to the Lord of the Mounted Hordes, and had to obey him lest the man slay the cat and so send his soul to Hell.

It was not a pleasant situation for the proud sorcerer, but he did not deserve less.

There was on the pale face of Elric of Melniboné some

slight trace of an earlier haunting, but his mouth smiled and his crimson eyes were at peace as he looked down at the young, black-haired woman with whom he walked in the terraced gardens of Karlaak.

'Elric,' said Zarozinia, 'have you found your happiness?'

He nodded. 'I think so. Stormbringer now hangs amid cobwebs in your father's armoury. The drugs I discovered in Troos keep me strong, my eyesight clear, and need to be taken only occasionally. I need never think of travelling or fighting again. I am content, here, to spend my time with you and study the books in Karlaak's library. What more would I require?'

'You compliment me overmuch, my lord. I would become complacent.'

He laughed. 'Rather that than you were doubting. Do not fear, Zarozinia, I possess no reason, now, to journey on. Moonglum, I miss, but it was natural that he should become restless of residence in a city and wish to revisit his homeland.'

'I am glad you are at peace, Elric. My father was at first reluctant to let you live here, fearing the black evil that once accompanied you, but three months have proved to him that the evil has gone and left no fuming berserker behind it.'

Suddenly there came a shouting from below them, in the street a man's voice was raised and he banged at the gates of the house.

'Let me in, damn you, I must speak with your master.'

A servant came running: 'Lord Elric – there is a man at the gates with a message. He pretends friendship with you.'

'His name?'

'An alien one – Moonglum, he says.'

'Moonglum! His stay in Elwher has been short. Let him in!'

Zarozinia's eyes held a trace of fear and she held Elric's arm fiercely. 'Elric – pray he does not bring news to take you hence.'

'No news could do that. Fear not, Zarozinia.' He hurried out of the garden and into the courtyard of the house. Moonglum rode hurriedly through the gates, dismounting as he did so.

'Moonglum, my friend! Why the haste? Naturally, I am pleased to see you after such a short time, but you have been riding hastily – why?'

The little Eastlander's face was grim beneath its coating of dust and his clothes were filthy from hard riding.

'The Flame Bringer comes with sorcery to aid him,' he panted. 'You must warn the city.'

'The Flame Bringer? The name means nothing – you sound delirious, my friend.'

'Aye, that's true, I am. Delirious with hate. He destroyed my homeland, killed my family, my friends and now plans conquests in the West. Two years ago he was little more than an ordinary desert raider but then he began to gather a great horde of barbarians around him and has been looting and slaying his way across the Eastern lands. Only Elwher has not suffered from his attacks, for the city was too great for even him to take. But he has turned two thousand miles of pleasant country into a burning waste. He plans world conquest, rides westwards with five hundred thousand warriors!'

'You mentioned sorcery – what does this barbarian know of such sophisticated arts?'

'Little himself, but he has one of our greatest wizards in his power – Drinij Bara. The man was captured as he lay drunk between two wenches in a tavern in Phum. He had put his soul into the body of a cat so that no rival sorcerer might steal it while he slept. But Terarn Gashtek, the Flame Bringer, knew of this trick, seized the cat and bound its legs, eyes and mouth, so imprisoning Drinij Bara's evil soul. Now the sorcerer is his slave – if he does not obey the barbarian, the cat will be killed by an iron blade and Drinij

102

Bara's soul will go to Hell.'

'These are unfamiliar sorceries to me,' said Elric. 'They seem little more than superstitions.'

'Who knows that they may be – but so long as Drinij Bara believes what he believes, he will do as Terarn Gashtek dictates. Several proud cities have been destroyed with the aid of his magic.'

'How far away is this Flame Bringer?'

'Three days' ride at most. I was forced to come hence by a longer route, to avoid his outriders.'

'Then we must prepare for a siege.'

'No, Elric – you must prepare to flee!'

'To flee – should I request the citizens of Karlaak to leave their beautiful city unprotected, to leave their homes?'

'If they will not – you must, and take your bride with you. None can stand against such a foe.'

'My own sorcery is no mean thing.'

'But one man's sorcery is not enough to hold back half a million men also aided by sorcery.'

'And Karlaak is a trading city – not a warrior's fortress. Very well, I will speak to the Council of Elders and try to convince them.'

'You must convince them quickly, Elric, for if you do not Karlaak will not stand half a day before Terarn Gashtek's howling blood-letters.'

'They are stubborn,' said Elric as the two sat in his private study later that night. 'They refuse to realize the magnitude of the danger. They refuse to leave and I cannot leave them for they have welcomed me and made me a citizen of Karlaak.'

'Then we must stay here and die?'

'Perhaps. There seems to be no choice. But I have another plan. You say that this sorcerer is a prisoner of Terarn Gashtek. What would he do if he regained his soul?'

'Why he would take vengeance upon his captor. But

103

Terarn Gashtek would not be so foolish as to give him the chance. There is no help for us there.'

'What if we managed to aid Drinij Bara?'

'How? It would be impossible.'

'It seems our only chance. Does this barbarian know of me or my history?'

'Not as far as I know.'

'Would he recognize you?'

'Why should he?'

'Then I suggest we join him.'

'Join him – Elric, you are no more sane than when we rode as free travellers together!'

'I know what I am doing. It would be the only way to get close to him and discover a subtle way to defeat him. We will set off at dawn, there is no time to waste.'

'Very well. Let's hope your old luck is good, but I doubt it now, for you've forsaken your old ways and the luck went with them.'

'Let us find out.'

'Will you take Stormbringer?'

'I had hoped never to have to make use of that hell-forged blade again. She's a treacherous sword at best.'

'Aye – but I think you'll need her in this business.'

'Yes, you're right. I'll take her.'

Elric frowned, his hands clenched. 'It will mean breaking my word to Zarozinia.'

'Better break it – than give her up to the Mounted Hordes.'

Elric unlocked the door to the armoury, a pitch torch flaring in one hand. He felt sick as he strode down the narrow passage lined with dulled weapons which had not been used for a century.

His heart pounded heavily as he came to another door and flung off the bar to enter the little room in which lay the disused regalia of Karlaak's long-dead War Chieftains –

and Stormbringer. The black blade began to moan, as if welcoming him as he took a deep breath of the musty air and reached for the sword. He clutched the hilt and his body was racked by an unholy sensation of awful ecstasy. His face twisted as he sheathed the blade and he almost ran from the armoury towards cleaner air.

Elric and Moonglum mounted their plainly equipped horses and, garbed like common mercenaries, bade urgent farewell to the Councillors of Karlaak.

Zarozinia kissed Elric's pale hand.

'I realize the need for this,' she said, her eyes full of tears, 'but take care, my love.'

'I shall. And pray that we are successful in whatever we decide to do.'

'The White Gods be with you.'

'No – pray to the Lords of the Darks, for it is their evil help I'll need in this work. And forget not my words to the messenger who is to ride to the south-west and find Dyvim Slorm.'

'I'll not forget,' she said, 'though I worry lest you succumb again to your old black ways.'

'Fear for the moment – I'll worry about my own fate later.'

'Then farewell, my lord, and be lucky.'

'Farewell, Zarozinia. My love for you will give me more power even than this foul blade here.' He spurred his horse through the gates and then they were riding for the Weeping Waste and a troubled future.

2

Dwarfed by the vastness of the softly turfed plateau which
was the Weeping Waste, the place of eternal rains, the two
horsemen drove their hard-pressed steeds through the
drizzle.

A shivering desert warrior, huddled against the weather,
saw them come towards him. He stared through the rain
trying to make out details of the riders, then wheeled his
stocky pony and rode swiftly back in the direction he had
come. Within minutes he had reached a larger group of
warriors attired like himself in furs and tasselled iron
helmets. They carried short bone bows and quivers of long
arrows fletched with hawk feathers. There were curved
scimitars at their sides.

He exchanged a few words with his fellows and soon they
were all lashing their horses towards the two riders.

'How much further lies the camp of Terarn Gashtek,
Moonglum?' Elric's words were breathless, for both men
had ridden for a day without halt.

'Not much further, Elric. We should be – look!'

Moonglum pointed ahead. About ten riders came swiftly
towards them. 'Desert barbarians – the Flame Bringer's
men. Prepare for a fight – they won't waste time parleying.'

Stormbringer scraped from the scabbard and the heavy
blade seemed to aid Elric's wrist as he raised it, so that it
felt almost weightless.

Moonglum drew both his swords, holding the short one
with the same hand with which he grasped his horse's reins.

The Eastern warriors spread out in a half circle as they
rode down on the companions, yelling wild war-shouts.
Elric reared his mount to a savage standstill and met the
first rider with Stormbringer's point full in the man's

throat. There was a stink like brimstone as it pierced flesh and the warrior drew a ghastly choking breath as he died, his eyes staring out in full realization of his terrible fate – for Stormbringer drank souls as well as blood.

Elric cut savagely at another desertman, lopping off his sword arm and splitting his crested helmet and the skull beneath. Rain and sweat ran down his white, taut features and into his glowing crimson eyes, but he blinked it aside, half-fell in his saddle as he turned to defend himself against another howling scimitar, parried the sweep, slid his own runeblade down its length, turned the blade with a movement of his wrist and disarmed the warrior. Then he plunged his sword into the man's heart and the desert warrior yelled like a wolf at the moon, a long baying shout before Stormbringer took his soul.

Elric's face was twisted in self-loathing as he fought intently with superhuman strength. Moonglum stayed clear of the albino's sword for he knew its liking for the lives of Elric's friends.

Soon only one opponent was left. Elric disarmed him and had to hold his own greedy sword back from the man's throat.

Reconciled to the horror of his death, the man said something in a guttural tongue which Elric half-recognized. He searched his memory and realized that it was a language close to one of the many ancient tongues which, as a sorcerer, he had been required to learn years before.

He said in the same language: 'Thou art one of the warriors of Terarn Gashtek the Flame Bringer.'

'That is true. And you must be the White-faced Evil One of legends. I beg you to slay me with a cleaner weapon than that which you hold.'

'I do not wish to kill thee at all. We were coming hence to join Terarn Gashtek. Take us to him.'

The man nodded hastily and clambered back on his horse.

'Who are you who speaks the High Tongue of our people?'

'I am called Elric of Melniboné – dost thou know the name?'

The warrior shook his head. 'No, but the High Tongue has not been spoken for generations, save by shamans – yet you're no shaman but, by your dress, seem a warrior.'

'We are both mercenaries. But speak no more. I will explain the rest to thy leader.'

They left a jackal's feast behind them and followed the quaking Easterner in the direction he led them.

Fairly soon, the low-lying smoke of many camp-fires could be observed and at length they saw the sprawling camp of the barbarian War Lord's mighty army.

The camp encompassed over a mile of the great plateau. The barbarians had erected skin tents on rounded frames and the camp had the aspect of a large primitive town. Roughly in the centre was a much larger construction, decorated with a motley assortment of gaudy silks and brocades.

Moonglum said in the Western tongue: 'That must be Terarn Gashtek's dwelling. See, he has covered its half-cured hides with a score of Eastern battle-flags.' His face grew grimmer as he noted the torn standard of Eshmir, the lion-flag of Okara and the blood-soaked pennants of sorrowing Changshai.

The captured warrior led them through the squatting ranks of barbarians who stared at them impassively and muttered to one another. Outside Terarn Gashtek's tasteless dwelling was his great war-lance decorated with more trophies of his conquests – the skulls and bones of Eastern princes and kings.

Elric said: 'Such a one as this must not be allowed to destroy the reborn civilization of the Young Kingdoms.'

'Young kingdoms are resilient,' remarked Moonglum, 'but it is when they are old that they fall – and it is often

108

Terarn Gashtek's kind that tear them down.'

'While I live he shall not destroy Karlaak – nor reach as far as Bakshaan.'

Moonglum said: 'Though, in my opinion, he'd be welcome to Nadsokor. The City of Beggars deserves such visitors as the Flame Bringer. If we fail, Elric, only the sea will stop him – and perhaps not that.'

'With Dyvim Slorm's aid – we shall stop him. Let us hope Karlaak's messenger finds my kinsman soon.'

'If he does not we shall be hard put to fight off half a million warriors, my friend.'

The barbarian shouted: 'Oh, Conqueror – mighty Flame Bringer – there are men here who wish to speak with you.'

A slurred voice snarled: 'Bring them in.'

They entered the badly smelling tent which was lighted by a fire flickering in a circle of stones. A gaunt man, carelessly dressed in bright captured clothing, lounged on a wooden bench. There were several women in the tent, one of whom poured wine into a heavy golden goblet which he held out.

Terarn Gashtek pushed the woman aside, knocking her sprawling and regarded the newcomers. His face was almost as fleshless as the skulls hanging outside his tent. His cheeks were sunken and his slanting eyes narrow beneath thick brows.

'Who are these?'

'Lord, I know not – but between them they slew ten of our men and would have slain me.'

'You deserved no more than death if you let yourself be disarmed. Get out – and find a new sword quickly or I'll let the shamans have your vitals for divination.' The man slunk away.

Terarn Gashtek seated himself upon the bench once more.

'So, you slew ten of my bloodletters, did you, and came here to boast to me about it? What's the explanation?'

'We but defended ourselves against your warriors – we sought no quarrel with them.' Elric now spoke the cruder tongue as best he could.

'You defended yourselves fairly well, I grant you. We reckon three soft-living house-dwellers to one of us. You are a Westerner, I can tell that, though your silent friend has the face of an Elwherite. Have you come from the East or the West?'

'The West,' Elric said, 'we are free travelling warriors, hiring our swords to those who'll pay or promise us good booty.'

'Are all Western warriors as skilful as you?' Terarn Gashtek could not hide his sudden realization that he might have under-estimated the men he hoped to conquer.

'We are a little better than most,' lied Moonglum, 'but not much.'

'What of sorcery – is there much strong magic here?'

'No,' said Elric, 'the art has been lost to most.'

The barbarian's thin mouth twisted into a grin, half of relief, half of triumph. He nodded his head, reached into his gaudy silks and produced a small black and white bound cat. He began to stroke its back. It wriggled but could do no more than hiss at its captor. 'Then we need not worry,' he said.

'Now, why did you come here? I could have you tortured for days for what you did, slaying ten of my best outriders.'

'We recognized the chance of enriching ourselves by aiding you, Lord Flame Bringer,' said Elric. 'We could show you the richest towns, lead you to ill-defended cities that would take little time to fall. Will you enlist us?'

'I've need of such men as you, true enough. I'll enlist you readily – but mark this, I'll not trust you until you've proved loyal to me. Find yourselves quarters now – and come to the feast, tonight. There I'll be able to show you something of the power I hold – the power which will smash the strength of the West and lay it waste for ten thousand miles.'

'Thanks,' said Elric. 'I'll look forward to tonight.'

They left the tent and wandered through the haphazard collection of tents and cooking fires, wagons and animals. There seemed little food, but wine was in abundance and the taut, hungry stomachs of the barbarians were placated with that.

They stopped a warrior and told him of Terarn Gashtek's orders to them. The warrior sullenly led them to a tent.

'Here – it was shared by three of the men you slew. It is yours by right of battle, as are the weapons and booty inside.'

'We're richer already,' grinned Elric with feigned delight.

In the privacy of the tent, which was less clean than Terarn Gashtek's, they debated.

'I feel uncommonly uncomfortable,' said Moonglum, 'surrounded by this treacherous horde. And every time I think of what they made of Eshmir, I itch to slay more of them. What now?'

'We can do nothing now – let us wait until tonight and see what develops.' Elric sighed. 'Our task seems impossible – I have never seen so great a horde as this.'

'They are invincible as they are,' said Moonglum. 'Even without Drinij Bara's sorcery to tumble down the walls of cities, no single nation could withstand them and, with the Western Nations squabbling among themselves, they could never unite in time. Civilization itself is threatened. Let us pray for inspiration – your dark gods are at least sophisticated, Elric, and we must hope that they'll resent the barbarian's intrusion as much as we do.'

'They play strange games with their human pawns,' Elric replied, 'and who knows what they plan?'

Terarn Gashtek's smoke-wreathed tent had been further

lighted by rush torches when Elric and Moonglum swaggered in, and the feast, consisting primarily of wine, was already in progress.

'Welcome, my friends,' shouted the Flame Bringer, waving his goblet. 'These are my captains – come, join them!'

Elric had never seen such an evil-looking group of barbarians. They were all half-drunk and, like their leader, had draped a variety of looted articles of clothing about themselves. But their swords were their own.

Room was made on one of the benches and they accepted wine which they drank sparingly.

'Bring in our slave!' yelled Terarn Gashtek. 'Bring in Drinij Bara our pet sorcerer.' Before him on the table lay the bound and struggling cat and beside it an iron blade.

Grinning warriors dragged a morose-faced man close to the fire and forced him to kneel before the barbarian chief. He was a lean man and he glowered at Terarn Gashtek and the little cat. Then his eyes saw the iron blade and his gaze faltered.

'What do you want with me now?' he said sullenly.

'Is that the way to address your master, spell-maker? Still, no matter. We have guests to entertain – men who have promised to lead us to fat merchant cities. We require you to do a few minor tricks for them.'

'I'm no petty conjurer. You cannot ask this of one of the greatest sorcerers in the world!'

'We do not ask – we order. Come, make the evening lively. What do you need for your magic-making? A few slaves – the blood of virgins? We shall arrange it.'

'I'm no mumbling shaman – I need no such trappings.'

Suddenly the sorcerer saw Elric. The albino felt the man's powerful mind tentatively probing his own. He had been recognized as a fellow sorcerer. Would Drinij Bara betray him?

Elric was tense, waiting to be denounced. He leaned

112

back in his chair and, as he did so, made a sign with his hand which would be recognized by Western sorcerers – would the Easterner know it?

He did. For a moment he faltered, glancing at the barbarian leader. Then he turned away and began to make new passes in the air, muttering to himself.

The beholders gasped as a cloud of golden smoke formed near the roof and began to metamorphose into the shape of a great horse bearing a rider which all recognized as Terarn Gashtek. The barbarian leader leaned forward, glaring at the image.

'What's this?'

A map showing great land areas and seas seemed to unroll beneath the horse's hooves. 'The Western lands,' cried Drinij Bara. 'I make a prophecy.'

'What is it?'

The ghostly horse began to trample the map. It split and flew into a thousand smoky pieces. Then the image of the horseman faded, also, into fragments.

'Thus will the mighty Flame Bringer rend the bountiful nations of the West,' shouted Drinij Bara.

The barbarians cheered exultantly, but Elric smiled thinly. The Eastern wizard was mocking Terarn Gashtek and his men.

The smoke formed into a golden globe which seemed to blaze and vanish.

Terarn Gashtek laughed. 'A good trick, magic-maker – and a true prophecy. You have done your work well. Take him back to his kennel!'

As Drinij Bara was dragged away, he glanced questioningly at Elric but said nothing.

Later that night, as the barbarians drank themselves into a stupor, Elric and Moonglum slipped out of the tent and made their way to the place where Drinij Bara was imprisoned.

They reached the small hut and saw that a warrior stood guard at the entrance. Moonglum produced a skin of wine and, pretending drunkenness, staggered towards the man. Elric stayed where he was.

'What do you want, Outlander?' growled the guard.

'Nothing, my friend, we are trying to get back to our own tent, that's all. Do you know where it is?'

'How should I know?'

'True – how should you? Have some wine – it's good – from Terarn Gashtek's own supply.'

The man extended a hand. 'Let's have it.'

Moonglum took a swig of the wine. 'No, I've changed my mind. It's too good to waste on common warriors.'

'Is that so?' The warrior took several paces towards Moonglum. 'We'll find out, won't we? And maybe we'll mix some of your blood with it to give it flavour, my little friend.'

Moonglum backed away. The warrior followed.

Elric ran softly towards the tent and ducked into it to find Drinij Bara, wrists bound, lying on a pile of uncured hides. The sorcerer looked up.

'You – what do you want?'

'We've come to aid you, Drinij Bara.'

'Aid me? But why? You're no friend of mine. What would you gain? You risk too much.'

'As a fellow sorcerer, I thought I'd help you,' Elric said.

'I thought you were that. But, in my land, sorcerers are not so friendly to one another – the opposite, in fact.'

'I'll tell you the truth – we need your aid to halt the barbarian's bloody progress. We have a common enemy. If we can help you regain your soul, will you help?'

'Help – of course. All I do is plan the way I'll avenge myself. But for my sake be careful – if he suspects that you're here to aid me, he'll slay the cat and slay us, too.'

'We'll try to bring the cat to you. Will that be what you need?'

'Yes. We must exchange blood, the cat and I, and my soul will then pass back into my own body.'

'Very well, I'll try to –' Elric turned, hearing voices outside. 'What's that?'

The sorcerer replied fearfully. 'It must be Terarn Gashtek – he comes every night to taunt me.'

'Where's the guard?' The barbarian's harsh voice came closer as he entered the little tent. 'What's . . .?' He saw Elric standing above the sorcerer.

His eyes were puzzled and wary. 'What are you doing here, Westerner – and what have you done with the guard?'

'Guard?' said Elric. 'I saw no guard. I was looking for my own tent and heard this cur cry out, so I entered. I was curious, anyway, to see such a great sorcerer clad in filthy rags and bound so.'

Terarn Gashtek scowled. 'Any more of such unwary curiosity, my friend, and you'll be discovering what your own heart looks like. Now, get hence – we ride on in the morning.'

Elric pretended to flinch and stumbled hurriedly from the tent.

A lone man in the livery of an Official Messenger of Karlaak goaded his horse southwards. The mount galloped over the crest of a hill and the messenger saw a village ahead. Hurriedly he rode into it, shouting at the first man he saw.

'Quickly, tell me – know you ought of Dyvim Slorm and his Imrryrian mercenaries? Have they passed this way?'

'Aye – a week ago. They went towards Rignariom by Jadmar's border, to offer their services to the Vilmirian Pretender.'

'Were they mounted or on foot?'

'Both.'

'Thanks, friend,' cried the messenger behind him and galloped out of the village in the direction of Rignariom.

The messenger from Karlaak rode through the night – rode along a recently made trail. A large force had passed that way. He prayed that it had been Dyvim Slorm and his Imrryrian warriors.

In the sweet-smelling garden city of Karlaak, the atmosphere was tense as the citizens waited for news they knew they could not expect for some time. They were relying on both Elric and on the messenger. If only one were successful, there would be no hope for them. Both had to be successful. Both.

3

The tumbling sound of moving men cut through the weeping morning and the hungry voice of Terarn Gashtek lashed at them to hurry.

Slaves packed up his tent and threw it into a wagon. He rode forward and wrenched his tall war-lance from the soft earth, wheeled his horse and rode westwards, his captains, Elric and Moonglum among them, behind him.

Speaking the Western tongue, Elric and Moonglum debated their problem. The barbarian was expecting them to lead him to his prey, his outriders were covering wide distances so that it would be impossible to lead him past a settlement. They were in a quandary for it would be disgraceful to sacrifice another township to give Karlaak a few days' grace, yet . . .

A little later two whooping outriders came galloping up to Terarn Gashtek.

'A town, lord! A small one and easy to take!'

'At last – this will do to test our blades and see how easy Western flesh is to pierce. Then we'll aim at a bigger target.' He turned to Elric: 'Do you know this town?'

'Where does it lie?' asked Elric thickly.

'A dozen miles to the south-west,' replied the outrider.

In spite of the fact that the town was doomed, Elric felt almost relieved. They spoke of the town of Gorjhan.

'I know it,' he said.

Cavim the Saddler, riding to deliver a new set of horse furniture to an outlying farm, saw the distant riders, their bright helmets caught by a sudden beam of sunlight. That the riders came from off the Weeping Waste was undoubtable – and he recognized menace in their massed progress.

He turned his mount about and rode with the speed of fear, back the way he had come to the town of Gorjhan.

The flat, hard mud of the street trembled beneath the thudding hooves of Cavim's horse and his high, excited shout knifed through shuttered windows.

'Raiders come! 'Ware the raiders!'

Within a quarter of an hour, the head-men of the town had met in hasty conference and debated whether to run or to fight. The older men advised their neighbours to flee the raiders, other younger men preferred to stay ready, armed to meet a possible attack. Some argued that their town was too poor to attract any raider.

The townspeople of Gorjhan debated and quarrelled, and the first wave of raiders came screaming to their walls.

With the realization that there was no time for further argument came the realization of their doom, and they ran to the ramparts with their pitiful weapons.

Terarn Gashtek roared through the milling barbarians who churned the mud around Gorjhan: 'Let's waste no time in siege. Fetch the sorcerer!'

They dragged Drinij Bara forward. From his garments, Terarn Gashtek produced the small black cat and held an iron blade at its throat.

'Work your spell, sorcerer, and tumble the walls quickly.'

The sorcerer scowled, his eyes seeking Elric, but the albino averted his own eyes and turned his horse away.

The sorcerer produced a handful of powder from his belt-pouch and hurled it into the air where it became first a gas, then a flickering ball of flame and finally a face, a dreadful unhuman face, formed in the flame.

'Dag-Gadden the Destroyer,' intoned Drinij Bara, 'you are sworn to our ancient pact – will you obey me?'

'I must, therefore I will. What do you command?'

'That you obliterate the walls of this town and so leave

118

the men inside naked, like crabs without their shells.'

'My pleasure is to destroy and destroy I shall.' The flaming face faded, altered, shrieked a searing course upward and became a blossoming scarlet canopy which hid the sky.

Then it swept down over the town and, in the instant of its passing, the walls of Gorjhan groaned, crumbled and vanished.

Elric shuddered – if Dag-Gadden came to Karlaak, such would be their fate.

Triumphant, the barbarian battlemongers swept into the defenceless town.

Careful to take no part in the massacre, Elric and Moonglum were also helpless to aid the slaughtered townspeople. The sight of the senseless, savage bloodshed around them enervated them. They ducked into a small house which seemed so far untouched by the pillaging barbarians. Inside they found three cowering children huddled around an older girl who clutched an old scythe in her soft hands. Shaking with fear, she prepared to stand them off.

'Do not waste our time, girl,' Elric said, 'or you'll be wasting your lives. Does this house have a loft?'

She nodded.

'Then get to it quickly. We'll make sure you're unharmed.'

They stayed in the house, hating to observe the slaughter-madness which had come upon the howling barbarians. They heard the dreadful sounds of carnage and smelled the stench of dead flesh and running blood.

A barbarian, covered in blood which was not his own, dragged a woman into the house by her hair. She made no attempt to resist, her face stunned by the horror she had witnessed.

Elric growled: 'Find another nest, hawk – we've made this our own.'

The man said: 'There's room enough here for what I want.'

Then, at last, Elric's clenched muscles reacted almost in spite of him. His right hand swung over to his left hip and the long fingers locked around Stormbringer's black hilt. The blade leapt from the scabbard as Elric stepped forward and, his crimson eyes blazing his sickened hatred, he smashed his sword down through the man's body. Unnecessarily, he clove again, hacking the barbarian in two. The woman remained where she lay, conscious but unmoving.

Elric picked up her inert body and passed it gently to Moonglum. 'Take her upstairs with the others,' he said brusquely.

The barbarians had begun to fire part of the town, their slaying all but done. Now they looted. Elric stepped out of the doorway.

There was precious little for them to loot but, still hungry for violence, they spent their energy on smashing inanimate things and setting fire to the broken, pillaged dwellings.

Stormbringer dangled loosely in Elric's hand as he looked at the blazing town. His face was a mask of shadow and frisking light as the fire threw up still longer tongues of flame to the misty sky.

Around him, barbarians squabbled over the pitiful booty; and occasionally a woman's scream cut above the other sounds, intermingled with rough shouts and the clash of metal.

Then he heard voices which were pitched differently to those in the immediate vicinity. The accents of the reavers mingled with a new tone –a whining, pleading tone. A group led by Terarn Gashtek came into view through the smoke.

Terarn Gashtek held something bloody in his hand – a human hand, severed at the wrist – and behind him swaggered several of his captains holding a naked old man between them. Blood ran over his body and gushed from his ruined arm, spurting sluggishly.

Terarn Gashtek frowned when he saw Elric. Then he shouted: 'Now, Westerner, you shall see how we placate our Gods with better gifts than meal and sour milk as this swine once did. He'll soon be dancing a pretty measure, I'll warrant – won't you, Lord Priest?'

The whining note went out of the old man's voice then and he stared with fever-bright eyes at Elric. His voice rose to a frenzied and high-pitched shriek which was curiously repellent.

'You dogs can howl over me!' he spat, 'but Mirath and T'aargano will be revenged for the ruin of their priest and their temple – you have brought flame here and you shall die by flame.' He pointed the bleeding stump of his arm at Elric – 'And you – you are a traitor and have been one in many causes, I can see it written in you. Though now . . . You are—' The priest drew breatn.

Elric licked his lips.

'I am what I am,' he said. 'And you are nothing but an old man soon to die. Your gods cannot harm us, for we do not pay them any respect. I'll listen no more to your senile meanderings!'

There was in the old priest's face all the knowledge of his past torment and the torment which was to come. He seemed to consider this and then was silent.

'Save your breath for screaming,' said Terarn Gashtek to the uncomprehending priest.

And then Elric said: 'It's bad luck to kill a priest, Flame Bringer!'

'You seem weak of stomach, my friend. His sacrifice to our own gods will bring us good luck, fear not.'

Elric turned away. As he entered the house again, a wild shriek of agony seared out of the night and the laughter which followed was not pleasant.

Later, as the still burning houses lit the night, Elric and Moonglum, carrying heavy sacks on their shoulders, clasping a woman each, moved with a simulation of drunkenness to the edge of the camp. Moonglum left the sacks and the women with Elric and went back, returning soon with three horses.

They opened the sacks to allow the children to climb out and watched the silent women mount the horses, aiding the children to clamber up.

Then they galloped away.

'Now,' said Elric savagely, 'we must work our plan tonight, whether the messenger reached Dyvid Slorm or not. I could not bear to witness another such sword-quenching.'

Terarn Gashtek had drunk himself insensible. He lay sprawled in an upper room of one of the unburned houses.

Elric and Moonglum crept towards him. While Elric watched to see that he was undisturbed, Moonglum knelt beside the barbarian leader and, lightfingered, cautiously reached inside the man's garments. He smiled in self-approval as he lifted out the squirming cat and replaced it with a stuffed rabbit-skin he had earlier prepared for the purpose. Holding the animal tight, he arose and nodded to Elric. Together, warily, they left the house and made their way through the chaos of the camp.

'I ascertained that Drinij Bara lies in the large wagon,' Elric told his friend. 'Quickly, now, the main danger's over.'

Moonglum said: 'When the cat and Drinij Bara have exchanged blood and the sorcerer's soul is back in his body – what then, Elric?'

'Together, our powers may serve at least to hold the barbarians back, but—' He broke off as a large group of warriors came weaving towards them.

'It's the Westerner and his little friend,' laughed one. 'Where are you off to, comrades?'

122

Elric sensed their mood. The slaughter of the day had not completely satiated their blood-lust. They were looking for trouble.

'Nowhere in particular,' he replied. The barbarians lurched around them, encircling them.

'We've heard much of your straight blade, stranger,' grinned their spokesman, 'and I'd a mind to test it against a real weapon.' He grabbed his own scimitar out of his belt. 'What do you say?'

'I'd spare you that,' said Elric coolly.

'You are generous – but I'd rather you accepted my invitation.'

'Let us pass,' said Moonglum.

The barbarians' faces hardened. 'Speak you so to the conquerors of the world?' said the leader.

Moonglum took a step back and drew his sword, the cat squirming in his left hand.

'We'd best get this done,' said Elric to his friend. He tugged his runeblade from its scabbard. The sword sang a soft and mocking tune and the barbarians heard it. They were disconcerted.

'Well?' said Elric, holding the half-sentient blade out.

The barbarian who had challenged him looked uncertain of what to do. Then he forced himself to shout: 'Clean iron can withstand any sorcery,' and launched himself forward.

Elric, grateful for the chance to take further vengeance, blocked his swing, forced the scimitar back and aimed a blow which sliced the man's torso just above the hip. The barbarian screamed and died. Moonglum, dealing with a couple more, killed one but another came in swiftly and his sweeping sword sliced the little Eastlander's left shoulder. He howled – and dropped the cat. Elric stepped in, slew Moonglum's opponent, Stormbringer wailing a triumphant dirge. The rest of the barbarians turned and ran off.

123

'How bad is your wound?' gasped Elric, but Moonglum was on his knees staring through the gloom.

'Quick, Elric – can you see the cat? I dropped it in the struggle. If we lose it – we too are lost.'

Frantically, they began to hunt through the camp.

But they were unsuccessful, for the cat, with the dexterity of its kind, had hidden itself.

A few moments later they heard the sounds of uproar coming from the house which Terarn Gashtek had commandeered.

'He's discovered that the cat's been stolen!' exclaimed Moonglum. 'What do we do now?'

'I don't know – keep searching and hope he does not suspect us.'

They continued to hunt, but with no result. While they searched, several barbarians came up to them. One of them said:

'Our leader wishes to speak with you.'

'Why?'

'He'll inform you of that. Come on.'

Reluctantly, they went with the barbarians to be confronted by a raging Terarn Gashtek. He clutched the stuffed rabbit skin in one claw-like hand and his face was warped with fury.

'My hold over the sorcerer has been stolen from me,' he roared. 'What do you know of it?'

'I don't understand,' said Elric.

'The cat is missing – I found this rag in its place. You were caught talking to Drinij Bara recently, I think you were responsible.'

'We know nothing of this,' said Moonglum.

Terarn Gashtek growled: 'The camp's in disorder, it will take a day to re-organize my men – once loosed like this they will obey no one. But when I've restored order, I shall question the whole camp. If you tell the truth, then you will be released, but meanwhile you will be given all the time you need to speak with the sorcerer.' He jerked his head. 'Take them away, disarm them, bind them and throw them in Drinij Bara's kennel.'

As they were led away, Elric muttered: 'We must escape and find that cat, but meanwhile we need not waste this opportunity to confer with Drinij Bara.'

Drinij Bara said in the darkness: 'No, Brother Sorcerer, I will not aid you. I will risk nothing until the cat and I are united.'

'But Terarn Gashtek cannot threaten you any more.'

'What if he recaptures the cat – what then?'

Elric was silent. He shifted his bound body uncomfortably on the hard boards of the wagon. He was about to continue his attempts at persuasion when the awning was thrown aside and he saw another trussed figure thrown towards them. Through the blackness he said in the Eastern tongue: 'Who are you?'

The man replied in the language of the West: 'I do not understand you.'

'Are you, then, a Westerner?' asked Elric in the common speech.

'Yes – I am an Official Messenger from Karlaak. I was captured by these odorous jackals as I returned to the city.'

'What? Are you the man we sent to Dyvim Slorm, my kinsman? I am Elric of Melniboné.'

'My lord, are we all, then, prisoners? Oh, gods – Karlaak is truly lost.'

'Did you get to Dyvim Slorm?'

'Aye – I caught up with him and his band. Luckily they were nearer to Karlaak than we suspected.'

'And what was his answer to my request?'

'He said that a few young ones might be ready, but even with sorcery to aid him it would take some time to get to the Dragon Isle. There is a chance.'

'A chance is all we need – but it will be no good unless

we accomplish the rest of our plan. Somehow Drinij Bara's soul must be regained so that Terarn Gashtek cannot force him to defend the barbarians. There is one idea I have – a memory of an ancient kinship that we of Melniboné had for a being called Meerclar. Thank the gods that I discovered those drugs in Troos and I still have my strength. Now, I must call my sword to me.'

He closed his eyes and allowed his mind and body first to relax completely and then concentrate on one single thing – the sword Stormbringer.

For years the evil symbiosis had existed between man and sword and the old attachments lingered.

He cried: Stormbringer! Stormbringer, unite with your brother! Come, sweet runeblade, come hell-forged kin-slayer, your master needs thee . . .'

Outside, it seemed that a wailing wind had suddenly sprung up. Elric heard shouts of fear and a whistling sound. Then the covering of the wagon was sliced apart to let in the starlight and the moaning blade quivered in the air over his head. He struggled upwards, already feeling nauseated at what he was about to do, but he was reconciled that he was not, this time, guided by self-interest but by the necessity to save the world from the barbarian menace.

'Give me thy strength, my sword,' he groaned as his bound hands grasped the hilt. 'Give me thy strength and let us hope it is for the last time.'

The blade writhed in his hands and he felt an awful sensation as its power, the power stolen vampire-like, from a hundred brave men, flowed into his shuddering body.

He became possessed of a peculiar strength which was not by any means wholly physical. His white face twisted as he concentrated on controlling the new power and the blade, both of which threatened to possess him entirely. He snapped his bonds and stood up.

126

Barbarians were even now running towards the wagon. Swiftly he cut the leather ropes binding the others and, unconscious of the nearing warriors, called a different name.

He spoke a new tongue, an alien tongue which normally he could not remember. It was a language taught to the Sorcerer Kings of Melniboné, Elric's ancestors, even before the building of Imrryr, the Dreaming City, over ten thousand years previously.

'Meerclar of the Cats, it is I, your kinsman, Elric of Melniboné, last of the line that made vows of friendship with you and your people. Do you hear me, Lord of the Cats?'

Far beyond the Earth, dwelling within a world set apart from the physical laws of space and time which governed the planet, glowing in a deep warmth of blue and amber, a manlike creature stretched itself and yawned, displaying tiny, pointed teeth. It pressed its head languidly against its furry shoulder – and listened.

The voice it heard was not that of one of its people, the kind he loved and protected. But he recognized the language.

He smiled to himself as remembrance came and he felt the pleasant sensation of fellowship. He remembered a race which, unlike other humans (whom he disdained) had shared his qualities – a race which, like him, loved pleasure, cruelty and sophistication for its own sake. The race of Melnibonéans.

Meerclar, Lord of the Cats, Protector of the Feline Kind, projected himself gracefully towards the source of the voice.

'How may I aid thee?' he purred.

'We seek one of your folk, Meerclar, who is somewhere close to here.'

'Yes, I sense him. What do you want of him?'

'Nothing which is his – but he has two souls, one of them not his own.'

'That is so – his name is Fiarshern of the great family of Trrechoww. I will call him. He will come to me.'

Outside, the barbarians were striving to conquer their fear of the supernatural events taking place in the wagon. Terarn Gashtek cursed them: 'There are five hundred thousand of us and a few of them. Take them now!'

His warriors began to move cautiously forward.

Fiarshern, the cat, heard a voice which it knew instinctively to be that of one which it would be foolish to disobey. It ran swiftly towards the source of that voice.

'Look – the cat – there it is. Seize it quickly.'

Two of Terarn Gashtek's men jumped forward to do his bidding, but the little cat eluded them and leaped lightly into the wagon.

'Give the human back its soul, Fiarshern,' said Meerclar softly. The cat moved towards its human master and dug its delicate teeth into the sorcerer's veins.

A moment later Drinij Bara laughed wildly. 'My soul is mine again. Thank you, great Cat Lord. Let me repay you!'

'There is no need,' smiled Meerclar mockingly, *'and, anyway, I perceive that your soul is already bartered. Goodbye, Elric of Melniboné. I was pleased to answer your call, though I see that you no longer follow the ancient pursuits of your fathers. Still, for the sake of old loyalties I do not begrudge you this service. Farewell, I go back to a warmer place than this inhospitable one.'*

The Lord of the Cats faded and returned to the world of blue and amber warmth where he once more resumed his interrupted sleep.

'Come, Brother Sorcerer,' cried Drinij Bara exultantly. 'Let us take the vengeance which is ours.'

He and Elric sprang from the wagon, but the two others were not quite so quick to respond.

Terarn Gashtek and his men confronted them. Many had bows with long arrows fitted to them.

128

'Shoot them down swiftly,' yelled the Flame Bringer. 'Shoot them now before they have time to summon further demons!'

A shower of arrows whistled towards them. Drinij Bara smiled, spoke a few words as he moved his hands almost carelessly. The arrows stopped in midflight, turned back and each uncannily found the throat of the man who had shot it. Terarn Gashtek gasped and wheeled back, pushing past his men and, as he retreated, shouted for them to attack the four.

Driven by the knowledge that if they fled they would be doomed, the great mass of barbarians closed in.

Dawn was bringing light to the cloud-ripped sky as Moonglum looked upwards. 'Look, Elric,' he shouted pointing.

'Only five,' said the albino. 'Only five – but perhaps enough.'

He parried several lashing blades on his own sword and, although he was possessed of superhuman strength, all the power seemed to have left the sword so that it was only as useful as an ordinary blade. Still fighting, he relaxed his body and felt the power leave him, flowing back into Stormbringer.

Again the runeblade began to whine and thirstily sought the throats and hearts of the savage barbarians.

Drinij Bara had no sword, but he did not need one, he was using subtler means to defend himself. All around him were the gruesome results, boneless masses of flesh and sinew.

The two sorcerers and Moonglum and the messenger forced their way through the half-insane barbarians who were desperately attempting to overcome them. In the confusion it was impossible to work out a coherent plan of action. Moonglum and the messenger grabbed scimitars from the corpses of the barbarians and joined in the battle.

Eventually, they had reached the outer limits of the camp. A whole mass of barbarians had fled, spurring their mounts westwards. Then Elric saw Terarn Gashtek, holding a bow. He saw the Flame Bringer's intention and shouted a warning to his fellow sorcerer who had his back to the barbarian. Drinij Bara, yelling some disturbing incantation, half-turned, broke off, attempted to begin another spell, but the arrow pierced his eye.

He screamed: *'No!'*

Then he died.

Seeing his ally slain, Elric paused and stared at the sky and the great wheeling beasts which he recognized.

Dyvim Slorm, son of Elric's cousin Dyvim Tvar the Dragon Master, had brought the legendary dragons of Imrryr to aid his kinsman. But most of the huge beasts slept, and would sleep for another century – only five dragons had been aroused. As yet, Dyvim Slorm could do nothing for fear of harming Elric and his comrades.

Terarn Gashtek, too, had seen the magnificent beasts. His grandiose plans of conquest were already fading and, thwarted, he ran towards Elric.

'You white-faced filth,' he howled, 'you have been responsible for all this – and you will pay the Flame Bringer's price!'

Elric laughed as he brought up Stormbringer to protect himself from the incensed barbarian. He pointed to the sky: 'These, too, can be called Flame Bringers. Terarn Gashtek – and are better named than thou!'

Then he plunged the evil blade full into Terarn Gashtek's body and the barbarian gave a choking moan as his soul was drawn from him.

'Destroyer, I may be, Elric of Melniboné,' he gasped, 'but my way was cleaner than yours. May you and all you hold dear be cursed for eternity!'

Elric laughed, but his voice shook slightly as he stared at the barbarian's corpse. 'I've rid myself of such curses once before, my friend. Yours will have little effect, I think.' He paused. 'By Arioch, I hope I'm right. I'd thought my fate cleansed of doom and curses, but perhaps I was wrong...'

The huge horde of barbarians were nearly all mounted now and fleeing westwards. They had to be stopped for, at the pace they were travelling, they would soon reach Karlaak and only the Gods knew what they would do when they got to the unprotected city.

Above him, he heard the flapping of thirty-foot wings and scented the familiar smell of the great flying reptiles which had pursued him years before when he had led a reaver fleet on the attack of his home-city. Then he heard the curious notes of the Dragon Horn and saw that Dyvim Slorm was seated on the back of the leading beast, a long spearlike goad in his gauntleted right hand.

The dragon spiralled downward and its great bulk came to rest on the ground thirty feet away, its leathery wings folding back along its length. The Dragon Master waved to Elric.

'Greetings, King Elric, we barely managed to arrive in time I see.'

'Time enough, kinsman,' smiled Elric. 'It is good to see the son of Dyvim Tvar again. I was afraid you might not answer my plea.'

'Old scores were forgotten at the Battle of Bakshaan when my father Dyvim Tvar died aiding you in the siege of Nikorn's fortress. I regret only the younger beasts were ready to be awakened. You'll remember the others were used but a few years past.'

'I remember,' said Elric. 'May I beg another favour, Dyvim Slorm?'

'What is that?'

'Let me ride the chief dragon. I am trained in the arts of the Dragon Master and have good reason for riding against the barbarians – we were forced to witness insensate carnage a while ago and may, perhaps, pay them back in their own coinage.'

Dyvim Slorm nodded and swung off his mount. The beast stirred restlessly and drew back the lips of its tapering snout to reveal teeth as thick as a man's arm, as long as a sword. Its forked tongue flickered and it turned its huge, cold eyes to regard Elric.

Elric sang to it in the old Melnibonéan speech, took the goad and the Dragon Horn from Dyvim Slorm and carefully climbed into the high saddle at the base of the dragon's neck. He placed his booted feet into the great silver stirrups.

'Now, fly, dragon brother,' he sang, 'up, up and have your venom ready.'

He heard the snap of displaced air as the wings began to beat and then the great beast was clear of the ground and soaring upwards into the grey and brooding sky.

The other four dragons followed the first and, as he gained height, sounding specific notes on the horn to give them directions, he drew his sword from its scabbard.

Centuries before, Elric's ancestors had ridden their dragon steeds to conquer the whole of the Western World. There had been many more dragons in the Dragon Caves in those days. Now only a handful remained, and of those only the youngest had slept sufficiently long enough to be awakened.

High in the wintry sky climbed the huge reptiles and Elric's long white hair and stained black cloak flew behind him as he sang the exultant *Song of the Dragon Masters* and urged his charges westwards.

> *Wild wind-horses soar the cloud-trails,*
> *Unholy horn doth sound its blast,*
> *You and we were first to conquer,*
> *You and we shall be the last!*

Thoughts of love, of peace, of vengeance even were lost in that reckless sweeping across the glowering skies which hung over that ancient Age of the Young Kingdoms. Elric, archetypal, proud and disdainful in his knowledge that even his deficient blood was the blood of the Sorcerer Kings of Melniboné, became detached.

He had no loyalties then, no friends and, if evil possessed him, then it was pure, brilliant evil, untainted by human drivings.

High soared the dragons until below them was the heaving black mass, marring the landscape, the fear-driven horde of barbarians who, in their ignorance, had sought to conquer the lands beloved of Elric of Melniboné.

'Ho, dragon brothers – loose your venom – burn – burn! And in your burning cleanse the world!'

Stormbringer joined in the wild shout and, diving, the dragons swept across the sky, down upon the crazed barbarians, shooting streams of combustible venom which water could not extinguish, and the stink of charred flesh drifted upwards through the smoke and flame so that the scene became a scene of Hell – and proud Elric was a Lord of Demons reaping awful vengeance.

He did not gloat, for he had done only what was needed, that was all. He shouted no more but turned his dragon mount back and upward, sounding his horn and summoning the other reptiles to him. And as he climbed the exultation left him and was replaced by cold horror.

'I am still a Melnibonéan,' he thought, 'and cannot rid myself of what else I do. And, in my strength I am still weak, ready to use this cursed blade in any small emergency.' With a shout of loathing, he flung the sword away, flung it into space. It screamed like a woman and went plummeting downwards towards the distant earth.

'There,' he said, 'it is done at last.' Then, in calmer

mood, he returned to where he had left his friends and guided his reptilian mount to the ground.

Dyvim Slorm said: 'Where is the sword of your forefathers, King Elric?' But the albino did not answer, just thanked his kinsman for the loan of the dragon leader. Then they all remounted the dragons and flew back towards Karlaak to tell them the news.

Zarozinia saw her lord riding the first dragon and knew that Karlaak and the Western World were saved, the Eastern World avenged. His stance was proud but his face was grave as he went to meet her outside the city. She saw in him a return of an earlier sorrow which he had thought forgotten. She ran to him and he caught her in his arms, holding her close but saying nothing.

He bade farewell to Dyvim Slorm and his fellow Imrryrians and, with Moonglum and the messenger following at a distance, went into the city and thence to his house, impatient of the congratulations which the citizens showered upon him.

'What is it, my lord?' Zarozinia said as, with a sigh, he sprawled wearily upon the great bed. 'Can speaking help?'

'I'm tired of swords and sorcery, Zarozinia, that is all. But at last I have rid myself once and for all of that hell-blade which I had thought my destiny to carry always.'

'Stormbringer you mean?'

'What else?'

She said nothing. She did not tell him of the sword which, apparently of its own volition, had come screaming into Karlaak and passed into the armoury to hang, in its old place, in darkness there.

He closed his eyes and drew a long, sighing breath.

'Sleep well, my lord,' she said softly. With tearful eyes and a sad mouth she lay herself down beside him.

She did not welcome the morning.

EPILOGUE

To Rescue Tanelorn . . .

In which we learn of the further adventures of Rackhir the Red Archer and other heroes and places Elric has hitherto encountered only in what he chooses to consider his dreams . . .

EPILOGUE
To Rescue Tanelorn . . .

Beyond the tall and ominous glass-green forest of Troos, well to the North and unheard of in Bakshaan, Elwher or any other city of the Young Kingdoms, on the shifting shores of the Sighing Desert lay Tanelorn, a lonely, long-ago city, loved by those it sheltered.

Tanelorn had a peculiar nature in that it welcomed and held the wanderer. To its peaceful streets and low houses came the gaunt, the savage, the brutalized, the tormented, and in Tanelorn they found rest.

Now, most of these troubled travellers who dwelt in peaceful Tanelorn had thrown off earlier allegiances to the Lords of Chaos who, as gods, took more than a mild interest in the affairs of men. It happened, therefore, that these same Lords grew to resent the unlikely city of Tanelorn and, not for the first time decided to act against it.

They instructed one of their number (more they could not, then, send) Lord Narjhan, to journey to Nadsokor, the City of Beggars, which had an old grudge against Tanelorn and raise an army that would attack undefended Tanelorn and destroy it and its inhabitants. So he did this, arming his ragged army and promising them many things.

Then, like a ferocious tide, did the beggar rabble set off to tear down Tanelorn and slay its residents. A great torrent of men and women in rags, on crutches, blind, maimed, but moving steadily, ominously, implacably Northwards towards the Sighing Desert.

In Tanelorn dwelt the Red Archer, Rackhir, from the Eastlands beyond the Sighing Desert, beyond the Weeping

Waste. Rackhir had been born a Warrior Priest, a servant of the Lords of Chaos, but had forsaken this life for the quieter pursuits of thievery and learning. A man with harsh features slashed from the bone of his skull, strong, fleshless nose, deep eye-cavities, a thin mouth and a thin beard. He wore a red skull-cap, decorated with a hawk's feather, a red jerkin, tight-fitting and belted at the waist, red breeks, and red boots. It was as if all the blood in him had transferred itself to his gear and left him drained. He was happy, however, in Tanelorn, the city which made all such men happy, and felt he would die there if men died there. He did not know if they did.

One day he saw Brut of Lashmar, a great, blond-headed noble of shamed name, ride wearily, yet urgently, through the low wall-gate of the city of peace. Brut's silver harness and trappings were begrimed, his yellow cloak torn and his broad-brimmed hat battered. A small crowd collected around him as he rode into the city square and halted. Then he gave his news.

'Beggars from Nadsokor, many thousands, move against our Tanelorn,' he said, 'and they are led by Narjhan of Chaos.'

Now, all the men in there were soldiers of some kind, good ones for the most part, and they were confident warriors, but few in number. A horde of beggars, led by such a being as Narjhan, could destroy Tanelorn, they knew.

'Should we, then, leave Tanelorn?' said Uroch of Nieva, a young, wasted man who had been a drunkard.

'We owe this city too much to desert her,' Rackhir said. 'We should defend her – for her sake and ours. There will never be such a city again.

Brut leaned forward in his saddle and said: 'In principle, Red Archer, I am in agreement with you. But principle is not enough without deeds. How would you suggest we defend this low-walled city against siege and the powers of Chaos?'

'We should need help,' Rackhir replied, 'supernatural help if need be.'

'Would the Grey Lords help us?' Zas the One-handed asked the question. He was an old, torn wanderer who had once gained a throne and lost it again.

'Aye – the Grey Lords!' Several voices chorused this hopefully.

'Who are the Grey Lords?' said Uroch, but no one heard him.

'They are not inclined to aid anyone at all,' Zas the One-handed pointed out, 'but surely Tanelorn, coming as it does under neither the Forces of Law nor the Lords of Chaos, would be worth their while preserving. After all, they have no loyalties either.'

'I'm for seeking the Grey Lords' aid,' Brut nodded. 'What of the rest of us?' There was general agreement, then silence when they realized that they knew of no means of contacting the mysterious and insouciant beings. At last Zas pointed this out.

Rackhir said: 'I know a seer – a hermit who lives in the Sighing Desert. Perhaps he can help?'

'I think that, after all, we should not waste time looking for supernatural assistance against this beggar rabble,' Uroch said. 'Let us prepare, instead, to meet the attack with physical means.'

'You forget,' Brut said wearily, 'that they are led by Narjhan of Chaos. He is not human and has the whole strength of Chaos behind him. We know that the Grey Lords are pledged neither to Law nor to Chaos but will sometimes help either side if the whim takes them. They are our only chance.'

'Why not seek the aid of the Forces of Law, sworn enemies of Chaos and mightier than the Grey Lords?' Uroch said.

139

'Because Tanelorn is a city owing alliegance to neither side. We are all of us men and women who have broken our pledge to Chaos but have made no new one to Law. The Forces of Law, in matters of this kind, will help only those sworn to them. The Grey Lords only may protect us, if they would.' So said Zas.

'I will go to find my seer,' Rackhir the Red Archer said, 'and if he knows how I may reach the Domain of the Grey Lords, then I'll continue straight on, for there is so little time. If I reach them and solicit their help you will soon know I have done so. If not, you must die in Tanelorn's defence and, if I live, I will join you in that last battle.'

'Very well,' Brut agreed, 'go quickly, Red Archer. Let one of your own arrows be the measure of your speed.'

And taking little with him save his bone bow and quiver of scarlet-fletched arrows, Rackhir set off for the Sighing Desert.

From Nadsokor, South West through the land of Vilmir, even through the squalid country of Org which has in it the dreadful forest of Troos, there was flame and black horror in the wake of the beggar horde, and insolent, disdainful of them though he led them, rode a being completely clad in black armour with a voice that rang hollow in the helm. People fled away at their approach and the land was made barren by their passing. Most knew what had happened, that the beggar citizens of Nadsokor had, contrary to their traditions of centuries, vomited from their city in a wild, menacing horde. Someone had armed them – someone had made them go Northwards and Westwards towards the Sighing Desert. But who was the one who led them? Ordinary folk did not know. And why did they head for the Sighing Desert? There was no city beyond Karlaak, which they had skirted, only the Sighing Desert – and beyond that the edge of the world. Was that their destination? Were they heading, lemming-like, to their destruction? Everyone hoped so, in their hate for the horrible horde.

Rackhir rode through the mournful wind of the Sighing Desert, his face and eyes protected against the particles of sand which flew about. He was thirsty and had been riding a day. Ahead of him at last were the rocks he sought.

He reached the rocks and called above the wind.

'Lamsar!'

The hermit came out in answer to Rackhir's shout. He was dressed in oiled leather to which sand clung. His beard, too, was encrusted with sand and his skin seemed to have taken on the colour and texture of the desert. He recognized Rackhir immediately, by his dress, beckoned him into the cave, and disappeared back inside. Rackhir dismounted and led his horse to the cave entrance and went in.

Lamsar was seated on a smooth rock. 'You are welcome, Red Archer,' he said, 'and I perceive by your manner that you wish information from me and that your mission is urgent.'

'I seek the help of the Grey Lords, Lamsar,' said Rackhir.

The old hermit smiled. It was as if a fissure had suddenly appeared in a rock. 'To risk the journey through the Five Gates, your mission must be important. I will tell you how to reach the Grey Lords, but the road is a difficult one.'

'I'm willing to take it,' Rackhir replied, 'for Tanelorn is threatened and the Grey Lords could help her.'

'Then you must pass through the First Gate, which lies in our own dimension. I will help you find it.'

'And what must I do then?'

'You must pass through all five gates. Each gateway leads to a realm which lies beyond and within our own

141

dimension. In each realm you must speak with the dwellers there. Some are friendly to men, some are not, but all must answer your question; "Where lies the next Gate?" though some may seek to stop you passing. The last gate leads to the Grey Lords' Domain.'

'And the first gate?'

'That lies anywhere in this realm. I will find it for you now.'

Lamsar composed himself to meditate and Rackhir, who had expected some sort of gaudy miracle-working from the old man, was disappointed.

Several hours went by until Lamsar said: 'The gate is outside. Memorize the following: If X is equal to the spirit of humanity, then the combination of the two must be of double power, therefore the spirit of humanity always contains the power to dominate itself.'

'A strange equation,' said Rackhir.

'Aye – but memorize it, meditate upon it and then we will leave.'

'We – you as well?'

'I think so.'

The hermit was old. Rackhir did not want him on the journey. But then he realized that the hermit's knowledge could be of use to him, so did not object. He thought upon the equation and, as he thought, his mind seemed to glitter and become diffused until he was in a strange trance and all his powers felt greater, both those of mind and body. The hermit got up and Rackhir followed him. They went out of the cave-mouth but, instead of the Sighing Desert, there was a hazy cloud of blue shimmering light ahead and when they had passed through this, in a second, they found themselves in the foothills of a low mountain-range and below them, in a valley, were villages. The villages were strangely laid out, all the houses in a wide circle about a huge amphitheatre containing, at its centre, a circular dais.

'It will be interesting to learn the reason why these villages are so arranged,' Lamsar said, and they began to move down into the valley.

As they reached the bottom and came close to one of the villages, people came gaily out and danced joyfully towards them. They stopped in front of Rackhir and Lamsar and, jumping from foot to foot as he greeted them, the leader spoke.

'You are strangers, we can tell – and you are welcome to all we have, food, accommodation, and entertainment.'

The two men thanked them graciously and accompanied them back to the circular village. The amphitheatre was made of mud and seemed to have been stamped out, hollowed into, the ground encompassed by the houses. The leader of the villagers took them to his house and offered them food.

'You have come to us at a Rest Time,' he said, 'but do not worry, things will soon commence again. My name is Yerleroo.'

'We seek the next Gate,' Lamsar said politely, 'and our mission is urgent. You will forgive us if we do not stay long?'

'Come,' said Yerleroo, 'things are about to commence. You will see us at our best, and must join us.'

All the villagers had assembled in the amphitheatre, surrounding the platform in the centre. Most of them were light-skinned and light-haired, gay and smiling, excited – but a few were evidently of a different race, dark, black-haired, and these were sullen.

Sensing something ominous in what he saw, Rackhir asked the question directly: 'Where is the next Gate?'

Yerleroo hesitated, his mouth worked and then he smiled. 'Where the winds meet,' he said.

Rackhir declared angrily: 'That's no answer.'

'Yes it is,' said Lamsar softly behind him. 'A fair answer.'

'Now we shall dance,' Yerleroo said. 'First you shall watch our dance and then you shall join in.'

'Dance?' said Rackhir, wishing he had brought a sword, or at least a dagger.

'Yes – you will like it. Everyone likes it. You will find it will do you good.'

'What if we do not wish to dance?'

'You must – it is for your own good, be assured.'

'And he –' Rackhir pointed at one of the sullen men. 'Does he enjoy it?'

'It is for his own good.'

Yerleroo clapped his hands and at once the fair-haired people leapt into a frenetic, senseless dance. Some of them sang. The sullen people did not sing. After a little hesitation, they began to prance dully about, their frowning features contrasting with their jerking bodies. Soon the whole village was dancing, whirling, singing a monotonous song.

Yerleroo flashed by, whirling. 'Come, join in now.'

'We had better leave,' Lamsar said with a faint smile. They backed away.

Yerleroo saw them. 'No – you must not leave – you must dance.'

They turned and ran as fast as the old man could go. The dancing villagers changed the direction of their dance and began to whirl menacingly towards them in a horrible semblance of gaiety.

'There's nothing for it,' Lamsar said and stood his ground, observing them through ironic eyes. 'The mountain gods must be invoked. A pity, for sorcery wearies me. Let us hope their magic extends to this plane. *Gordar!*'

Words in an unusually harsh language issued from Lamsar's old mouth. The whirling villagers came on.

144

Lamsar pointed at them.

The villagers became suddenly petrified and slowly disturbingly, their bodies caught in a hundred positions, turned to smooth black basalt.

'It was for their own good,' Lamsar smiled grimly. 'Come, to the place where the winds meet,' and he took Rackhir there quite swiftly.

At the place where the winds met they found the second gateway, a column of amber-coloured flame, shot through with streaks of green. They entered it and, instantly, were in a world of dark, seething colour. Above them was a sky of murky red in which other colours shifted, agitated, changing. Ahead of them lay a forest, dark, blue, black, heavy, mottled green, the tops of its trees moving like a wild tide. It was a howling land of unnatural phenomena.

Lamsar pursed his lips. 'On this plane Chaos rules, we must get to the next gate swiftly for obviously the Lords of Chaos will seek to stop us.'

'Is it always like this?' Rackhir gasped.

'It is always boiling midnight – but the rest, it changes with the moods of the Lords. There are no rules at all.'

They pressed on through the bounding, blossoming scenery as it erupted and changed around them. Once they saw a huge winged figure in the sky, smoky yellow, and roughly man-shaped.

'Vezhan,' Lamsar said, 'let's hope he did not see us.'

'Vezhan!' Rackhir whispered the name – for it was to Vezhan that he had once been loyal.

They crept on, uncertain of their direction or even of their speed in that disturbing land.

At length, they came to the shores of a peculiar ocean.

It was a grey, heaving, timeless sea, a mysterious sea which stretched into infinity. There could be no other shores beyond this rolling plain of water. No other lands or rivers or dark, cool woods, no other men or women or ships. It was a sea which led to nowhere. It was complete to itself – a sea.

Over this timeless ocean hovered a brooding ochre sun which cast moody shadows of black and green across the water, giving the whole scene something of the look of being enclosed in a vast cavern, for the sky above was gnarled and black with ancient clouds. And all the while the doom-carried crash of breakers, the lonely, fated monotony of the ever-rearing white-topped waves; the sound which portended neither death nor life nor war nor peace – simply existence and shifting inharmony. They could go no further.

'This has the air of our death about it,' Rackhir said shivering.

The sea roared and tumbled, the sound of it increasing to a fury, daring them to go on towards it, welcoming them with wild temptation – offering them nothing but achievement – the achievement of death.

Lamsar said: 'It is not my fate wholly to perish.' But then they were running back towards the forest, feeling that the strange sea was pouring up the beach towards them. They looked back and saw that it had gone no further, that the breakers were less wild, the sea more calm. Lamsar was a little way behind Rackhir.

The Red Archer gripped his hand and hauled him towards him as if he had rescued the old man from a whirlpool. They remained there, mesmerized, for a long time, while the sea called to them and the wind was a cold caress on their flesh.

In the bleak brightness of the alien shore, under a sun which gave no heat, their bodies shone like stars in the night and they turned towards the forest, quietly.

'Are we trapped, then, in this Realm of Chaos?' Rackhir said at length. 'If we meet someone, they will offer us harm – how can we ask our question?'

Then there emerged from the huge forest a great figure, naked and gnarled like the trunk of a tree, green as lime, but the face was jovial.

'Greetings, unhappy renegades,' it said.

'Where is the next gate?' said Lamsar quickly.

'You almost entered it, but turned away,' laughed the giant. 'That sea does not exist – it is there to stop travellers from passing through the gate.'

'It exists here, in the Realm of Chaos,' Rackhir said thickly.

'You could say so – but what exists in Chaos save the disorders of the minds of gods gone mad?'

Rackhir had strung his bone bow and fitted an arrow to the string, but he did it in the knowledge of his own hopelessness.

'Do not shoot the arrow,' said Lamsar softly. 'Not yet.' And he stared at the arrow and muttered.

The giant advanced carelessly towards them, unhurried.

'It will please me to exact the price of your crimes from you,' it said, 'for I am Hionhurn the Executioner. You will find your death pleasant – but your fate unbearable.' And he came closer, his clawed hands outstretched.

'Shoot!' croaked Lamsar and Rackhir brought the bow-string to his cheek, pulled it back with might and released the arrow at the giant's heart. 'Run!' cried Lamsar, and in spite of their forebodings they ran back down the shore towards the frightful sea. They heard the giant groan behind them as they reached the edge of the sea and, instead of running into water, found themselves in a range of stark mountains.

'No mortal arrow could have delayed him,' Rackhir said. 'How did you stop him?'

'I used an old charm – the Charm of Justice, which when applied to any weapon, makes it strike at the unjust.'

147

'But why did it hurt Hionhurn, an immortal?' Rackhir asked.

'There is no justice in the world of Chaos – something constant and inflexible, whatever its nature, must harm any servant of the Lords of Chaos.'

'We have passed through the third gate,' Rackhir said, unstringing his bow, 'and have the fourth and fifth to find. Two dangers have been avoided – but what new ones will we encounter now?'

'Who knows?' said Lamsar, and they walked on through the rocky mountain pass and entered a forest that was cool, even though the sun had reached its zenith and was glaring down through parts of the thick foliage. There was an air of ancient calm about the place. They heard unfamiliar bird-calls and saw tiny golden birds which were also new to them.

'There is something calm and peaceful about this place – I almost distrust it,' Rackhir said, but Lamsar pointed ahead silently.

Rackhir saw a large domed building, magnificent in marble and blue mosaic. It stood in a clearing of yellow grass and the marble caught the sun, flashing like fire.

They neared the domed construction and saw that it was supported by big marble columns set into a platform of milky jade. In the centre of the platform, a stairway of blue-stone curved upwards and disappeared into a circular aperture. There were wide windows set into the sides of the raised building but they could not see inside. There were no inhabitants visible and it would have seemed strange to the pair if there had been. They crossed the yellow glade and stepped on to the jade platform. It was warm, as if it had been exposed to the sun. They almost slipped on the smooth stone.

They reached the blue steps and mounted them, staring upwards, but they could still see nothing. They did not attempt to ask themselves why they were so assuredly invading the building; it seemed quite natural that they should do what they were doing. There was no alternative. There was an air of familiarity about the place. Rackhir felt it but did not know why. Inside was a cool, shadowy hall, a blend of soft darkness and bright sunlight which entered by the windows. The floor was pearl-pink and the ceiling deep scarlet. The hall reminded Rackhir of a womb.

Partially hidden by deep shadow was a small doorway and beyond it, steps. Rackhir looked questioningly at Lamsar. 'Do we proceed in our exploration?'

'We must – to have our question answered, if possible.'

They climbed the steps and found themselves in a smaller hall similar to the one beneath them. This hall, however, was furnished with twelve wide thrones placed in a semicircle in the centre. Against the wall, near the door, were several chairs, upholstered in purple fabric. The thrones were of gold, decorated with fine silver, padded with white cloth.

A door behind the thrones opened and a tall, fragile-looking man appeared, followed by others whose faces were almost identical. Only their robes were noticeably different. Their faces were pale, almost white, their noses straight, their lips thin but not cruel. Their eyes were unhuman – green-flecked eyes which stared outwards with sad composure. The leader of the tall men looked at Rackhir and Lamsar. He nodded and waved a pale, long-fingered hand gracefully.

'Welcome,' he said. His voice was high and frail, like a girl's, but beautiful in its modulation. The other eleven men seated themselves in the thrones but the first man, who had spoken, remained standing. 'Sit down, please,' he said.

Rackhir and Lamsar sat down on two of the purple chairs.

149

'How did you come here?' enquired the man.

'Through the gates from Chaos,' Lamsar replied.

'And were you seeking our realm?'

'No – we travel towards the Domain of the Grey Lords.'

'I thought so, for your people rarely visit us save by accident.'

'Where are we?' asked Rackhir as the man seated himself in the remaining throne.

'In a place beyond time. Once our land was part of the earth you know, but in the dim past it became separated from it. Our bodies, unlike yours, are immortal. We choose this, but we are not bound to our flesh, as you are.'

'I don't understand,' frowned Rackhir. 'What are you saying?'

'I have said what I can in the simplest terms understandable to you. If you do not know what I say then I can explain no further. We are called the Guardians – though we guard nothing. We are warriors, but we fight nothing.'

'What else do you do?' enquired Rackhir.

'We exist. You will want to know where the next gateway lies?'

'Yes.'

'Refresh yourselves here, and then we shall show you the gateway.'

'What is your function?' asked Rackhir.

'To function,' said the man.

'You are unhuman!'

'We are human. *You* spend your lives chasing that which is within you and that which you can find in any other human being – but you will not look for it there – you must follow more glamorous paths – to waste your time in order to discover that you have wasted your time.

I am glad that we are no longer like you – but I wish that it were lawful to help you further. This, however, we may not do.'

'Ours is no meaningless quest,' said Lamsar quietly, with respect. 'We go to rescue Tanelorn.'

'Tanelorn?' the man said softly. 'Does Tanelorn still remain?'.

'Aye,' said Rackhir, 'and shelters tired men who are grateful for the rest she offers.' Now he realized why the building had been familiar – it had the same quality, but intensified, as Tanelorn.

'Tanelorn was the last of our cities,' said the Guardian. 'Forgive us for judging you – most of the travellers who pass through this plane are searchers, restless, with no real purpose, only excuses, imaginary reasons for journeying on. You must love Tanelorn to brave the dangers of the gateways?'

'We do,' said Rackhir, 'and I am grateful that you built her.'

'We built her for ourselves, but it is good that others have used her well – and she them.'

'Will you help us?' Rackhir said. 'For Tanelorn?'

'We cannot – it is not lawful. Now, refresh yourselves and be welcome.'

The two travellers were given foods, both soft and brittle, sweet and sour, and drink which seemed to enter the pores of their skin as they quaffed it, and then the Guardian said: 'We have caused a road to be made. Follow it and enter the next world. But we warn you, it is the most dangerous of all.'

And they set off down the road that the Guardians had caused to be made and passed through the fourth gateway into a dreadful realm – the Realm of Law.

Nothing shone in the grey-lit sky, nothing moved,

151

nothing marred the grey.

Nothing interrupted the bleak grey plain stretching on all sides of them, forever. There was no horizon. It was a bright, clean wasteland. But there was a sense about the air, a presence of something past, something which had gone but left a faint aura of its passing.

'What dangers could be here?' said Rackhir shuddering, 'here where there is nothing?'

'The danger of the loneliest madness,' Lamsar replied. Their voices were swallowed in the grey expanse.

'When the Earth was very young,' Lamsar continued, his words trailing away across the wilderness, 'things were like this – but there were seas, there were seas. Here there is nothing.'

'You are wrong,' Rackhir said with a faint smile. 'I have thought – here there is Law.'

'That is true – but what is Law without something to decide between? Here is Law – bereft of justice.'

They walked on, all about them an air of something intangible that had once been tangible. On they walked through this barren world of Absolute Law.

Eventually, Rackhir spied something. Something that flickered, faded, appeared again until, as they neared it, they saw that it was a man. His great head was noble, firm, and his body was massively built, but the face was twisted in a tortured frown and he did not see them as they approached him.

They stopped before him and Lamsar coughed to attract his attention. He turned that great head and regarded them abstractedly, the frown clearing at length, to be replaced by a calmer, thoughtful expression.

'Who are you?' asked Rackhir.

The man sighed. 'Not yet,' he said, 'not yet, it seems. More phantoms.'

'Are *we* the phantoms?' smiled Rackhir. 'That seems to

be more your own nature.' He watched as the man began slowly to fade again, his form less definite, melting. The body seemed to make a great heave, like a salmon attempting to leap a dam, then it was back again in a more solid form.

'I had thought myself rid of all that was superfluous, save my own obstinate shape,' the man said tiredly, 'but here is something, back again. Is my reason failing – is my logic no longer what it was?'

'Do not fear,' said Rackhir, 'we are material beings.'

'That is *what* I feared. For an eternity I have been stripping away the layers of unreality which obscure the truth. I have almost succeeded in the final act, and now you begin to creep back. My mind is not what it was, I think.'

'Perhaps you worry lest we do not exist?' Lamsar said slowly, with a clever smile.

'You know that is not so – you do not exist, just as I do not exist.' The frown returned, the features twisted, the body began, again, to fade, only to resume, once more, its earlier nature. The man sighed. 'Even to reply to you is betraying myself, but I suppose a little relaxation will serve to rest my powers and equip me for the final effort of will which will bring me to the ultimate truth – the truth of non-being.'

'But non-being involves non-thought, non-will, non-action,' Lamsar said. 'Surely you would not submit yourself to such a fate?'

'There is no such thing as self. I am the only reasoning thing in creation – I am almost pure reason. A little more effort and I shall be what I desire to be – the one truth in this non-existent universe. That requires first ridding myself of anything extraneous around me – such as yourselves – and then making the final plunge into the only reality.'

'What is that?'

153

'The state of absolute nothingness where there is nothing to disturb the order of things because there *is* no order of things.'

'Scarcely a constructive ambition,' Rackhir said.

'Construction is a meaningless word – like all words, like all so-called existence. Everything means nothing – that is the only truth.'

'But what of this world? Barren as it is, it still has light and firm rock. You have not succeeded in reasoning that out of existence,' Lamsar said.

'That will cease when I cease,' the man said slowly, 'just as you will cease to be. Then there can be nothing but nothing and Law will reign unchallenged.'

'But Law cannot reign – it will not exist either, according to your logic.'

'You are wrong – nothingness is the Law. Nothingness is the object of Law. Law is the way to its ultimate state, the state of non-being.'

'Well,' said Lamsar musingly, 'then you had better tell us where we may find the next gate.'

'There is no gate.'

'If there were, where would we find it?' Rackhir said.

'If a gate existed, and it does not, it would have been inside the mountain, close to what was once called the Sea of Peace.'

'And where was that?' Rackhir asked, conscious, now, of their terrible predicament. There were no landmarks, no sun, no stars – nothing by which they could determine direction.

'Close to the Mountain of Severity.'

'Which way do you go?' Lamsar enquired of the man.

'Out – beyond – to nowhere.'

'And where, if you succeed in your object, will *we* be consigned?'

'To some other nowhere. I cannot truthfully answer. But since you have never existed in reality, therefore you can go on to no non-reality. Only I am real – and I do not exist.'

'We are getting nowhere,' said Rackhir with a smirk which changed to a frown.

'It is only my mind which holds the non-reality at bay,' the man said, 'and I must concentrate or else it will all come flooding back and I shall have to start from the beginning again. In the beginning, there was everything – Chaos. I *created* nothing.'

With resignation, Rackhir strung his bow, fitted an arrow to the string and aimed at the frowning man.

'You wish for non-being?' he said.

'I have told you so.' Rackhir's arrow pierced his heart, his body faded, became solid and slumped to the grass as mountains, forests, and rivers appeared around them. It was still a peaceful, well-ordered world and Rackhir and Lamsar, as they strode on in search of the Mountain of Severity, savoured it. There seemed to be no animal life here and they talked, in puzzled terms, about the man they had been forced to kill, until, at length they reached a great smooth pyramid which seemed, though it was of natural origin, to have been carved into this form. They walked around its base until they discovered an opening.

There could be no doubt that this was the Mountain of Severity, and a calm ocean lay some distance away. They went into the opening and emerged into a delicate landscape. They were now through the last gateway and in the Domain of the Grey Lords.

There were trees like stiffened spider-webs.

Here and there were blue pools, shallow, with shining water and graceful rocks balanced in them and around their shores. Above them and beyond them the light hills swept away towards a pastel yellow horizon which was tinted with red, orange, and blue, deep blue.

They felt overlarge, clumsy, like crude, gross giants

155

treading on the fine, short grass. They felt as if they were destroying the sanctity of the place.

Then they saw a girl come walking towards them.

She stopped as they came closer to her. She was dressed in loose black robes which flowed about her as if in a wind, but there was no wind. Her face was pale and pointed, her black eyes large and enigmatic. At her long throat was a jewel.

'Sorana,' said Rackhir thickly, 'you died.'

'I disappeared,' said she, 'and this is where I came. I was told that you would come to this place and decided that I would meet you.'

'But this is the Domain of the Grey Lords – and you serve Chaos.'

'I do – but many are welcome at the Grey Lords' Court, whether they be of Law, Chaos, or neither. Come, I will escort you there.'

Bewildered, now, Rackhir let her lead the way across the strange terrain and Lamsar followed him.

Sorana and Rackhir had been lovers once, in Yesh-potoom-Kahlai, the Unholy Fortress, where evil blossomed and was beautiful. Sorana, sorceress, adventuress, was without conscience but had had high regard for the Red Archer since he had come to Yeshpotoom-Kahlai one evening, covered in his own blood, survivor of a bizarre battle between the Knights of Tumbru and Loheb Bakra's brigand-engineers. Seven years ago, that had been, and he had heard her scream when the Blue Assassins had crept into the Unholy Fortress, pledged to murder evil-makers. Even then he had been in the process of hurriedly leaving Yeshpotoom-Kahlai and had considered it unwise to investigate what was obviously a death-scream. Now she was here – and if she was here, then it was for a strong reason and for her own convenience. On the other hand, it was in her interests to serve Chaos and he must be

156

suspicious of her.

Ahead of them now they saw many great tents of shimmering grey which, in the light, seemed composed of all colours. People moved slowly among the tents and there was an air of leisure about the place.

'Here,' Sorana said, smiling at him and taking his hand, 'the Grey Lords hold impermanent court. They wander about their land and have few artefacts and only temporary houses which you see. They will make you welcome if you interest them.'

'But will they help us?'

'You must ask them.'

'You are pledged to Eequor of Chaos,' Rackhir observed, 'and must aid her against us, is that not so?'

'Here,' she smiled, 'is a truce. I can only inform Chaos of what I learn of your plans and, if the Grey Lords aid you, must tell them how, if I can find out.'

'You are frank, Sorana.'

'Here there are subtler hypocrisies – and the subtlest lie of all is the full truth,' she said, as they entered the area of tall tents and made their way towards a certain one.

In a different realm of the Earth, the huge horde careered across the grasslands of the North, screaming and singing behind the black-armoured horseman, their leader. Nearer and nearer they came to lonely Tanelorn, their motley weapons shining through the evening mists. Like a boiling tidal wave of insensate flesh, the mob drove on, hysterical with the hate for Tanelorn which Narjhan had placed in their thin hearts. Thieves, murderers, jackals, scavengers – a scrawny horde, but huge . . .

And in Tanelorn the warriors were grim-faced as their outriders and scouts flowed into the city with messages and estimates of the beggar army's strength.

Brut, in the silver armour of his rank, knew that two full days had passed since Rackhir had left for the Sighing

Desert. Three more days and the city would be engulfed by Narjhan's mighty rabble – and they knew there was no chance of halting their advance. They might have left Tanelorn to its fate, but they would not. Even weak Uroch would not. For Tanelorn the Mysterious had given them all a secret power which each believed to be his only, a strength which filled them where before they had been hollow men. Selfishly, they stayed – for to leave Tanelorn to her fate would be to become hollow again, and that they all dreaded.

Brut was the leader and he prepared the defence of Tanelorn – a defence which might just have held against the beggar army – but not against it and Chaos. Brut shuddered when he thought that if Chaos had directed its full force against Tanelorn, they would be sobbing in Hell at that moment.

Dust rose high above Tanelorn, sent flying by the hooves of the scouts' and messengers' horses. One came through the gate as Brut watched. He pulled his mount to a stop before the nobleman. He was the messenger from Kaarlak, by the Weeping Waste, one of the nearest major cities to Tanelorn.

The messenger gasped: 'I asked Kaarlak for aid but, as we supposed, they had never heard of Tanelorn and suspected that I was an emissary from the beggar army sent to lead their few forces into a trap. I pleaded with the Senators, but they would do nothing.'

'Was not Elric there – he knows Tanelorn?'

'No, he was not there. There is a rumour which says that he himself fights Chaos now, for the minions of Chaos captured his wife Zarozinia and he rides in pursuit of them. Chaos, it seems, gains strength everywhere in our realm.'

Brut was pale.

'What of Jadmar – will Jadmar send warriors?' The

messenger spoke urgently, for many had been sent to the nearer cities to solicit aid.

'I do not know,' replied Brut, 'and it does not matter now – for the beggar army is not three days' march from Tanelorn and it would take two weeks for a Jadmarian force to reach us.'

'And Rackhir?'

'I have heard nothing and he has not returned. I have the feeling he will not return. Tanelorn is doomed.'

Rackhir and Lamsar bowed before the three small men who sat in the tent, but one of them said impatiently: 'Do not humble yourselves before us, friends – we who are humbler than any.' So they straightened their backs and waited to be further addressed.

The Grey Lords assumed humility, but this, it seemed, was their greatest ostentation, for it was a pride that they had. Rackhir realized that he would need to use subtle flattery and was not sure that he could, for he was a warrior, not a courtier or a diplomat. Lamsar, too, realized the situation and he said:

'In our pride, Lords, we have come to learn the simpler truths which are only truths – the truths which you can teach us.'

The speaker gave a self-deprecating smile and replied: 'Truth is not for us to define, guest, we can but offer our incomplete thoughts. They might interest you or help you to find your own truths.'

'Indeed, that is so,' Rackhir said, not wholly sure with what he was agreeing, but judging it best to agree. 'And we wondered if you had any suggestions on a matter which concerns us – the protection of our Tanelorn.'

'We would not be so prideful as to interfere our own comments. We are not mighty intellects,' the speaker replied blandly, 'and we have no confidence in our own decisions, for who knows that they may be wrong and based on wrongly assessed information?'

'Indeed,' said Lamsar, judging that he must flatter them with their own assumed humility, 'and it is lucky for us, Lords, that we do not confuse pride with learning – for it is the quiet man who observes and says little who sees the most. Therefore, though we realize that you are not confident that your suggestions or help would be useful, none the less we, taking example from your own demeanour, humbly ask if you know of any way in which we might rescue Tanelorn?'

Rackhir had hardly been able to follow the complexities of Lamsar's seemingly unsophisticated argument, but he saw that the Grey Lords were pleased. Out of the corner of his eye he observed Sorana. She was smiling to herself and it seemed evident, by the characteristics of that smile, that they had behaved in the right way. Now Sorana was listening intently and Rackhir cursed to himself that the Lords of Chaos would know of everything and might, even if they did gain the Grey Lords' aid, still be able to anticipate and stop any action they took to save Tanelorn.

The speaker conferred in a liquid speech with his fellows and said finally: 'Rarely do we have the privilege to entertain such brave and intelligent men. How may our insignificant minds be put to your advantage?'

Rackhir realized quite suddenly, and almost laughed, that the Grey Lords were not very clever after all. Their flattery had got them the help they required. He said:

'Narjhan of Chaos heads a huge army of human scum – a beggar army – and is sworn to tear down Tanelorn and kill her inhabitants. We need magical aid of some kind to combat one so powerful as Narjhan *and* defeat the beggars.'

'But Tanelorn cannot be destroyed . . .' said a Grey

Lord. 'She is Eternal...' said another. 'But this manifestation...' murmured the third. 'Ah, yes...'

'There are beetles in Kaleef,' said a Grey Lord who had not spoken before, 'which emit a peculiar venom.'

'Beetles, Lord?' said Rackhir.

'They are the size of mammoths,' said the third Lord, 'but can change their size – and change the size of their prey if it is too large for their gullets.'

'As for that matter,' the first speaker said, 'there is a chimera which dwells in mountains South of here – it can change its shape and contains hate for Chaos since Chaos bred it and abandoned it with no real shape of its own.'

'Then there are four brothers of Himerscahl who are endowed with sorcerous power,' said the second Lord, but the first interrupted him:

'Their magic is no good outside our own dimension,' he said. 'I had thought, however, of reviving the Blue Wizard.'

'Too dangerous and, anyway, beyond our powers,' said his companion.

They continued to debate for a while, and Rackhir and Lamsar said nothing, but waited.

Eventually the first speaker said:

'The Boatmen of Xerlerenes, we have decided, will probably be best equipped to aid you in defence of Tanelorn. You must go to the mountains of Xerlerenes and find their lake.'

'A lake,' said Lamsar, 'in a range of mountains, I see.'

'No,' the Lord said, 'their lake lies above the mountains. We will find someone to take you there. Perhaps they will aid you.'

'You can guarantee nothing else?'

'Nothing – it is not our business to interfere. It is up to them to decide whether they will aid you or not.'

'I see,' said Rackhir, 'thank you.'

161

How much time had passed since he had left Tanelorn? How much time before Narjhan's beggar army reached the city? Or had it already done so?

Suddenly he thought of something, looked for Sorana, but she had left the tent.

'Where lies Xerlerenes?' Lamsar was asking.

'Not in our realm,' one of the Grey Lords replied, 'come we will find you a guide.'

Sorana spoke the necessary word which took her immediately into the blue half-world with which she was so familiar. There were no other colours in it, but many, many shades of blue. Here she waited until Eequor noticed her presence. In the timelessness, she could not tell how long she had waited.

The beggar horde came to an undisciplined and slow halt at a sign from its leader. A voice rang hollowly from the helm that was always closed.

'*Tomorrow, we march against Tanelorn – the time we have anticipated is almost upon us. Make camp now. Tomorrow shall Tanelorn be punished and the stones of her little houses will be dust on the wind.*'

The million beggars cackled their glee and wetted their scrawny lips. Not one of them asked why they had marched so far, and this was because of Narjhan's power.

In Tanelorn, Brut and Zas the One-handed discussed the nature of death in quiet, over-controlled tones. Both were filled with sadness, less for themselves than for Tanelorn, soon to perish. Outside, a pitiful army tried to place a cordon around the town but failed to fill the gaps between men, there were so few of them. Lights in the houses burned as if for the last time, and candles guttered moodily.

Sorana, sweating as she always did after such an episode,

returned to the plane occupied by the Grey Lords and discovered that Rackhir, Lamsar, and their guide were preparing to leave. Eequor had told her what to do – it was for her to contact Narjhan. The rest the Lords of Chaos would accomplish. She blew her ex-lover a kiss as he rode from the camp into the night. He grinned at her defiantly, but when his face was turned from her he frowned and they went in silence into the Valley of the Currents where they entered the world where lay the Mountains of Xerlerenes. Almost as soon as they arrived, danger presented itself.

Their guide, a wanderer called Timeras, pointed into the night sky which was spiked by the outlines of crags.

'This is a world where the air elementals are dominant,' he said. 'Look!'

Flowing downwards in an ominous sweep they saw a flight of owls, great eyes gleaming. Only as they came nearer did the men realize that these owls were huge, almost as large as a man. In the saddle Rackhir strung his bow. Timeras said:

'How could they have learned of our presence so soon?'

'Sorana,' Rackhir said, busy with the bow, 'she must have warned the Lords of Chaos and they have sent these dreadful birds.' As the first one homed in, great claws grasping, great beak gaping, he shot it in its feathery throat and it shrieked and swept upwards. Many arrows fled from his humming bow-string to find a mark while Timeras drew his sword and slashed at them, ducking as they whistled downwards.

Lamsar watched the battle but took no part, seemed thoughtful at a time when action was desired of him.

He mused: 'If the spirits of air are dominant in this world, then they will resent a stronger force of other elementals,' and he racked his brain to remember a spell.

Rackhir had but two arrows left in his quiver by the

163

time they had driven the owls off. The birds had not been used, evidently, to a prey which fought back and had put up a poor fight considering their superiority.

'We can expect more danger,' said Rackhir somewhat shakily, 'for the Lords of Chaos will use other means to try and stop us. How far to Xerlerenes?'

'Not far,' said Timeras, 'but it's a hard road.'

They rode on, and Lamsar rode behind them, lost in his own thoughts.

Now they urged their horses up a steep mountain path and a chasm lay below them, dropping, dropping, dropping. Rackhir, who had no love for heights, kept as close to the mountainside as was possible. If he had had gods to whom he could pray, he would have prayed for their help then.

The huge fish came flying – or swimming – at them as they rounded a bend. They were semi-luminous, big as sharks but with enlarged fins with which they planed through the air like rays. They were quite evidently fish. Timeras drew his sword, but Rackhir had only two arrows left and it would have been useless against the air-fish to have shot them, for there were many of the fish.

But Lamsar laughed and spoke in a high-pitched, staccato speech. '*Crackhor – pishtasta salaflar!*'

Huge balls of flame materialized against the black sky – flaring balls of multicoloured fire which shaped themselves into strange, warlike forms and streamed towards the unnatural fish.

The flame-shapes seared into the big fish and they shrieked, struck at the fire-balls, burned, and fell flaming down the deep gorge.

'Fire elementals!' Rackhir exclaimed.

'The spirits of the air fear such beings,' Lamsar said calmly.

The flame-beings accompanied them the rest of the way

to Xerlerenes and were with them when dawn came, having frightened away many other dangers which the Lords of Chaos had evidently sent against them.

They saw the boats of Xerlerenes in the dawn, at anchor on a calm sky, fluffy clouds playing around their slender keels, their huge sails furled.

'The boatmen live aboard their vessels,' Timeras said, 'for it is only their ships which deny the laws of nature, not they.'

Timeras cupped his hands about his mouth and called through the still mountain air: 'Boatmen of Xerlerenes, freemen of the air, guests come with a request for aid!'

A black and bearded face appeared over the side of one of the red-gold vessels. The man shielded his eyes against the rising sun and stared down at them. Then he disappeared again.

At length a ladder of slim thongs came snaking down to where they sat their horses on the tops of the mountains. Timeras grasped it, tested it and began to climb. Rackhir reached out and steadied the ladder for him. It seemed too thin to support a man but when he had it in his hands he knew that it was the strongest he had ever known.

Lamsar grumbled as Rackhir signalled for him to climb, but he did so and quite nimbly. Rackhir was the last, following his companions, climbing up through the sky high above the crags, towards the ship that sailed on the air.

The fleet comprised some twenty or thirty ships and Rackhir felt that with these to aid him, there was a good chance to rescue Tanelorn – if Tanelorn survived. Narjhan would, anyway, be aware of the nature of the aid he sought.

Starved dogs barked the morning in and the beggar

horde, walking from where they had sprawled on the ground, saw Narjhan already mounted, but talking to a newcomer, a girl in black robes that moved as if in a wind – but there was no wind. There was a jewel at her long throat.

When he had finished conversing with the newcomer, Narjhan ordered a horse be brought for her and she rode slightly behind him when the beggar army moved on – the last stage of their hateful journey to Tanelorn.

When they saw lovely Tanelorn and how it was so poorly guarded, the beggars laughed, but Narjhan and his new companion looked up into the sky.

'*There may be time*,' said the hollow voice, and gave the order to attack.

Howling, the beggars broke into a run towards Tanelorn. The attack had started.

Brut rose in his saddle and there were tears flowing down his face and glistening in his beard. His huge war-axe was in one gauntleted hand and the other held a spiked mace across the saddle before him.

Zas the One-handed gripped the long and heavy broadsword with its pommel of a rampant golden lion pointed downwards. This blade had won him a crown in Andlermaigne, but he doubted whether it would successfully defend his peace in Tanelorn. Beside him stood Uroch of Nieva, pale-faced but angry as he watched the ragged horde's implacable approach.

Then, yelling, the beggars met with the warriors of Tanelorn and, although greatly outnumbered, the warriors fought desperately for they were defending more than life or love – they were defending that which had told them of a reason for living.

Narjhan sat his horse aside from the battle, Sorana next to him, for Narjhan could take no active part in the battle, could only watch and, if necessary, use magic to aid his human pawns or defend his person.

The warriors of Tanelorn, incredibly, held back the roaring beggar horde, their weapons drenched with blood, rising and falling in that sea of moving flesh, flashing in the light of the red dawn.

Sweat now mingled with the salt tears in Brut's bristling beard and with agility he leapt clear of his black horse as the screaming beast was cut from under him. The noble war-cry of his forefathers sang on his breath and, although in his shame he had no business to use it, he let it roar from him as he slashed about him with biting war-axe and rending mace. But he fought hopelessly for Rackhir had not come and Tanelorn was soon to die. His one fierce consolation was that he would die with the city, his blood mingling with its ashes.

Zas, also, acquitted himself very well before he died of a smashed skull. His old body twitched as trampling feet stumbled over it as the beggars made for Uroch of Nieva. The gold-pommelled sword was still gripped in his single hand and his soul was fleeing for Limbo as Uroch, too, was slain fighting.

Then the Ships of Xerlerenes suddenly materialized in the sky and Brut, looking upward for an instant, knew that Rackhir had come at last – though it might be too late.

Narjhan, also, saw the Ships and was prepared for them.

They skimmed through the sky, the fire elementals which Lamsar had summoned, flying with them. The spirits of air and flame had been called to rescue weakening Tanelorn . . .

The Boatmen prepared their wagons and made themselves ready for war. Their black faces had a concentrated look and they grinned in their bushy beards. War-harness clothed them and they bristled with weapons – long, barbed tridents, nets of steel mesh, curved swords, long harpoons. Rackhir stood in the prow of the leading ship, his quiver packed with slim arrows loaned him by the Boatmen. Below him he saw Tanelorn and was relieved that the city still stood.

He could see the milling warriors below, but it was hard to tell, from the air, which were friends and which were foes. Lamsar called to the frisking fire elementals, instructing them. Timeras grinned and held his sword ready as the ships rocked in the wind and dropped lower.

Now Rackhir observed Narjhan with Sorana beside him.

'The bitch has warned him – he is ready for us,' Rackhir said, wetting his lips and drawing an arrow from his quiver.

Down the Ships of Xerlerenes dropped, coursing downwards on the currents of air, their golden sails billowing, the warrior crews straining over the side and keen for battle.

Then Narjhan summoned the *Kyrenee*.

Huge as a storm-cloud, black as its native Hell, the *Kyrenee* grew from the surrounding air and moved its shapeless bulk forward towards the Ships of Xerlerenes, sending out flowing tendrils of poison towards them. Boatmen groaned as the coils curled around their naked bodies and crushed them.

Lamsar called urgently to his fire elementals and they rose again from where they had been devouring beggars, came together in one great blossoming of flame which moved to do battle with the *Kyrenee*.

The two masses met and there was an explosion which blinded the Red Archer with multi-coloured light and sent the Ships rocking and shaking so that several capsized and sent their crews hurtling downwards to death.

Blotches of flame flew everywhere and patches of poison blackness from the body of the *Kyrenee* were flung about, slaying those they touched before disappearing.

There was a terrible stink in the air – a smell of burning, a smell of outraged elements which had never been meant to meet.

The *Kyrenee* died, lashing about and wailing, while the flame elementals, dying or returning to their own sphere, faded and vanished. The remaining bulk of the great *Kyrenee* billowed slowly down to the earth where it fell upon the scrabbling beggars and killed them, leaving nothing but a wet patch on the ground for yards around, a patch glistening with the bones of beggars.

Now Rackhir cried: 'Quickly – finish the fight before Narjhan summons more horrors!'

And the boats sailed downwards while the Boatmen cast their steel nets, pulling large catches of beggars aboard their ships and finishing the wriggling starvelings with their tridents and spears.

Rackhir shot arrow after arrow and had the satisfaction of seeing each one take a beggar just where he had aimed it. The remaining warriors of Tanelorn, led by Brut who was covered in sticky blood but grinning in his victory, charged towards the unnerved beggars.

Narjhan stood his ground, while the beggars, fleeing, streamed past him and the girl. Sorana seemed frightened, looked up and her eyes met Rackhir's. The Red Archer aimed an arrow at her, thought better of it and shot instead at Narjhan. The arrow went into the black armour but had no effect upon the Lord of Chaos.

Then the Boatmen of Xerlerenes flung down their largest net from the vessel in which Rackhir sailed and they caught Lord Narjhan in its coils and caught Sorana, too.

Shouting their exhilaration, they pulled the struggling

bodies aboard and Rackhir ran forward to inspect their catch. Sorana had received a scratch across her face from the net's wire, but the body of Narjhan lay still and dreadful in the mesh.

Rackhir grabbed an axe from a Boatman and knocked back the helm, his foot upon the chest.

'Yield, Narjhan of Chaos!' he cried in mindless merriment. He was near hysterical with victory, for this was the first time a mortal had ever bested a Lord of Chaos.

But the armour was empty, if it had even been occupied by flesh, and Narjhan was gone.

Calm settled aboard the Ships of Xerlerenes and over the city of Tanelorn. The remnants of the warriors had gathered in the city's square and were cheering their victory.

Friagho, the Captain of Xerlerenes, came up to Rackhir and shrugged. 'We did not get the catch we came for – but these will do. Thanks for the fishing, friend.'

Rackhir smiled and gripped Friagho's black shoulder. 'Thanks for the aid – you have done us all a great service.'

Friagho shrugged again and turned back to his nets, his trident poised. Suddenly Rackhir shouted: 'No, Friagho – let that one be. Let me have the contents of that net.'

Sorano, the contents to which he'd referred, looked anxious as if she had rather been transfixed on the prongs of Friagho's trident. Friagho said: 'Very well, Red Archer – there are plenty more people on the land,' pulled at the net to release her.

She stood up shakily, looking at Rackhir apprehensively.

Rackhir smiled quite softly and said: 'Come here, Sorana.' She went to him and stood staring up at his bony hawk's face, her eyes wide. With a laugh he picked her up and flung her over his shoulder.

'Tanelorn is safe!' he shouted. 'You shall learn to love its peace with me!' And he began to clamber down the trailing ladders that the Boatmen had dropped over the side.

Lamsar waited for him below. 'I go now, to my hermitage again.'

'I thank you for your aid,' said Rackhir. 'Without it Tanelorn would no longer exist.'

'Tanelorn will always exist while men exist,' said the hermit. 'It was not a city you defended today. It was an ideal. That is Tanelorn.'

And Lamsar smiled.